MW01226026

# THE BEAUTY MAN

Stuart Richmond

To my dearest Emma
with much love
from
Dad xy

Copyright @ 2022 Stuart Richmond

Stuart Richmond has asserted his right under the Copyright Design and Patents Act, 1988 to be identified as the author of the work.

All rights reserved. No part of this publication may be reproduced, stored in a retrieval system, or transmitted in any form or by any means without prior written permission, nor be otherwise circulated in any form of binding or cover other than that in which it is published and without similar conditions being imposed on the subsequent purchaser.

This novel is a work of fiction and the characters, organizations and places herein are drawn from the author's imagination. Any resemblance these characters, organizations and places may have to real persons, living or dead, organizations and places is entirely coincidental.

ISBN-9798428771190

# Dedication

For Mandy

# 1

Caspar was in the shower groaning a little. His prostate was aching. Not enough to stop him from getting on with things but enough to give him pause to be grateful to ibuprofen. He had to be careful not to overdo it with the scotch or the little gland could swell, become inflamed and reduce his flow of urine to a painful trickle. The urologist had advised him not to have the surgery to remove it because of some unpalatable side effects such as no erection. Even the medication to shrink it could cause him to have swollen breasts. He could have it reamed out but that seemed to him to be bloody and a bit medieval. The specialist had recommended frequent ejaculation but even that was a bit off the radar now. So he stuck it out trying to be sensible. Strong red wines, scotch and caffeinated coffee were off the menu mostly. White wines and everything decaf were his main options. But then nobody could be good all the time. Right now he was letting the hot water spray soothingly between his buttocks. Caspar at sixty-eight, was around six feet tall and weighed 190 lbs. He was dark haired with a few grey streaks and his body was covered all over with fine dark hair. Caspar was living alone. Marjorie, his wife of almost forty years had died in her sleep nearly two years ago. She'd had a heart attack and was already cold when he woke up.

For Caspar she was always the lovely vivacious girl he had met at Cambridge: Blonde-haired, willowy and with an unabashed Yorkshire accent to go with her working-class origins in Sheffield. He had lain there bereft, arms wrapped tightly around her, wet faced, whispering little talisman words to her, kissing her, repeating her name, his head resting in her neck, refusing to believe she was gone. In some vaguely aware niche of his mind he felt the oft-expressed truth that the gods didn't like us to be too happy.

He'd stayed beside her for several hours before calling the ambulance. The paramedics needed to pull him away from her. For days after he was unable to move, emotionally shattered, sitting in the living room, drinking scotch, unwashed, not eating, bleary, just out of it. Only now after months of heartache was he more or less sleeping through the night, not waking up first thing to inquire whether she wanted tea.

They had hiked many miles together in Western Canada over the years, especially in the Okanagan valley and up and down the west coast exploring the majestic Coastal Range of mountains and the Gulf Islands. They loved identifying and reading up on natural history and local culture. In Vancouver they had enjoyed movies, followed the Baroque Ensemble, and gone on frequent visits to Toronto and London to attend concerts, go to exhibitions, visit bookshops, and enjoy long city treks just exploring. Unable to have children, they'd kept trying. This was before the days of IVF. She had been an integral part of his being for so long. Laughing at him, loving him, supporting him through some rough patches but always together. They were very lucky and knew it but did not suffer from hubris. It was a simple life. In the early days Caspar wondered whether she would have liked to pursue an academic career. But she was adamant. She wanted to work with children.

Marjorie had retired a few years ago at age sixty-two as a high school social studies teacher and was free and keen on their sojourns. She had more recently been teaching an archeology course at a local college. She grew up in a small terraced house near the steel mill where her dad worked. Her mother didn't work outside the home. But her parents always supported her love of books and learning. She had gone on to an all girls' grammar school, wearing the uniform of green blazer, skirt and beret, stockings to the knee, and the famous elasticated flannel "passion killers" they had always laughed about.

Then, by a miracle, she had been accepted at Cambridge University to study history, receiving a grant to support her there.

Marjorie had a natural grace that won people over. Caspar met her at the Arts Society dance and watched her in debate at the union. She was quick on her feet, eloquent, and quite left leaning. She was also a member of the Rock Climbing Club going off into Derbyshire and Wales on weekends. He asked her out. She turned him down. That's how they got started.

Now, this morning, letting the water do its thing, Caspar, namely Dr. Caspar Logan Ballantyne, professor of aesthetic and moral philosophy at Vancouver University, was having a gripe to himself about the latest Faculty demand for his learning objectives. More admin trivia. The University, the oldest in western Canada, small at six thousand students and sitting on fifty acres of prime city land adjacent to the harbor, had been the nearest thing to an ivy league school in its day. It was still highly regarded as a top liberal arts university. The campus was replete with its original moss-covered granite and gothic style buildings and landscaped grounds, paid for a century ago by local timber merchants and city fathers wanting something to lift the city above its smoky, muddy, rambunctious rail terminus image — a kind of Harvard of the Pacific. It was a jewel of a setting that would do credit to Capability Brown, but even now was being eyed by the Province and city fathers given the astronomical property prices and the increasing weight of opinion as to the general uselessness of the degrees.

Caspar was a bit of a one-off. He'd fought the good fight over the years to defend the liberal arts program and had been head of philosophy twice, a job nobody wanted, or at least nobody you would want wanted. He worked alone, taught well and took on mad projects such as his recent book on aesthetic appreciation, which had been a surprising best seller both within and outside of academe. He still smoked a pipe on occasion, and was pretty decent to colleagues and students but would fight his corner when provoked. What was the point of tenure if it did not give you the balls to stand up for the good, the true, and the beautiful? Amazingly, there were still some people in this crazy world who believed in such things. Most of his colleagues though kept their heads down not wanting anything to get in the way of their career progress. Tenure for many of them meant a job for life. Being a prof was not a bad sinecure. Yet plans were afoot to replace the arts and humanities with more digital and business subjects. The administration felt this would save the university from attacks of irrelevance and a rumored reduction in government funding.

Caspar knew his aesthetics program would be at risk when he retired, after all what university program could be seen as more useless. But for Caspar the whole idea of the aesthetic, of engaging with things for their own sakes, for their intrinsic value, was essential for life. And he wanted to see his two remaining grad students complete their doctorates before leaving. At this stage he decided to ignore the administration's constant demands for professors to develop their own websites, promote themselves on social media, and make Ted Talks. Selfishly he did none of these things. Given his publication record he did his own thing risking being mugged by the salary and tenure committee. He had good contacts with a couple of National Institutes of Art in China where he went periodically to teach and hang out with colleagues there. One of his favourite books was the venerable Tao te Ching. He never tired of reading it. It had given him succor in the aftermath of Marjorie's death.

As a student he had gone from Canada to do a doctorate in philosophy on a scholarship to Cambridge. This was in the early seventies. He had been taught by ex-students of Wittgenstein, once regarded as the most notable philosopher of the twentieth century, and he had loved the whole experience. He had learned to work out the logical geography of ideas as they used to say, focusing on language and the arts. Caspar carried on in his own work identifying and making arguments regarding what values were of most worth. He kept asking how are we best to live, educate, think, feel, be, respond, in what kind of moral and aesthetic universe? How to preserve and nourish one's unique self? Drawing upon what sources of spiritual value? He resisted talk of thinking skills, keeping instead with the imprecision of understanding, imagination, and feeling as the hallmarks of mind. And all this set against the power of media indoctrination, technology, and marketing.

He was just about coping with life at this point living in their one hundred year old apartment filled with art—paintings by Canadian artists such as Greg Hardy, a classical Chinese landscape or two, bits of nature such as leaves, stones, driftwood and seashells and many of his own photographs, mainly landscapes and some portraits, a calligraphic scroll by brush and black ink--a gift for his work in China, and pieces of local and Japanese ceramics etc., etc. A large worn pale red fabric sofa long enough to stretch out on and sink into when reading by the fire and a scuffed tan leather armchair next to it were his main places of refuge, plus his study, of course. Everything was old, vintage even, including the old non-electronic GE fridge and stove. The apartment had fifteen-foot high ceilings with ogee mouldings, cast iron radiators, a large unvarnished pine table in the kitchen, and the blessing of a bidet in the bathroom courtesy of the Italian developer.

In the early days of bereavement the apartment, once a place of well being for Caspar, a place where his life experience had played out and been so enriched with Marjorie, had lost much of its meaning.

Traces of her were of course everywhere including her scent, Chanel no 5, and yet she was, irrevocably, gone. And as her memory seemed to drain imperceptibly out of his life so too he felt his marriage, once his emotional mainstay, become a chimera. Music had been one of their loves yet he found he couldn't listen to the Romantic repertoire any more. Now it seemed overblown, needing some intellectual salt, to be found for him in

Bach and other baroque composers, their music played on original instruments.

In the early days following Marjorie's death, Adele, their longstanding cleaning lady, you could say went beyond the call of duty in finding him more than once drunk and asleep on the living room carpet and getting him upright and ready for the day. She kept up an air of brisk normality admonishing him where needed, keeping him supplied with clean clothes and a stocked refrigerator, and on a couple of occasions she had held him while he cried.

He dreamed of earlier times, so real, calling out to Marjorie in a summer frock receding down an old university corridor, there but always out of reach. Then he would wake up, realizing. This past year alone three of his friends had died. A university friend Gustav from lymphoma, an old friend Sarah, an American who had taught high school with Marjorie, whom he had loved for her sprezzatura and attitude, and his once high school girlfriend, Monica, a dark-haired musician and swimmer, both from cancer.

Caspar's parents now deceased had grown up on sheep farms in Northumberland close to the Scottish border. But times were hard after the war. They had immigrated to Canada and landed up in Vancouver in 1952. Caspar was four years old. Dad Ted, who had fought in the Italian Campaign and walked with a limp due to a shrapnel wound in his left knee, had gone to UBC and qualified as an engineer. His mother, Eileen a dark haired borders girl had attended art college and trained as a painter, a profession in which she had found some success. Her work as a portraitist was popular. She and Ted walked a lot and went ballroom dancing at the community centre on Sundays, taking family holidays on the Gulf Islands and the Okanagan, a fruit-growing valley astride a seventy-mile long lake. They had lived on the West Side in a small 1920s house with basement back door to a garden with fruit trees and a vegetable patch. The whole block had been planted with ash trees, which by now were quite mature.

His mother was the gardener. She had encouraged his interest in the arts taking him to concerts and exhibitions as he grew up. There was a steady flow of letters to and from his grandparents on both sides. This was pre zoom and phone calls were expensive. Nor could people fly across the Atlantic as readily as they do now. So he had some contact and birthday presents and stories from his parents about their lives growing up on farms but not much face-to-face contact.

Caspar had walked to school at Kitsilano High, played rugby at wing forward and had loved everything academic but also his art classes. He went to UBC for a degree in philosophy and visual art working all through university to help pay his expenses. Time off was spent swimming and playing volleyball off Kits beach. He could remember feeling a girl's breasts in the park one night in great wonder and making love for the first time among the washed up logs. There were no drugs back then apart from some pot the hippies were growing. Funny how as we age comes an urge to know what happened to friends and the people we loved. Little things can set us off. Finding a lost photograph for example: the shine in a girl's eyes, her youth, that smile. What was she thinking? Who was she looking at? The body, remembering.

Caspar, you could say, had become a caricature of the aging professor, now part of an earlier generation. And he had come to some firm convictions about life and academe. He was, however, with age, if anything more creative and open, encouraging his philosophy students to be more personal and subjective. Their work could include for example, poetry and photographs. A thesis had to be scholarly but it could also be expressive. The world, Caspar knew, could not be captured in linguistic analysis alone. Matters of the soul required voice, style, touch, ways of being, metaphor, gesture, poetry, a passage in a concerto, a dance movement, a painting, or a view from a city bus in the evening light. Beauty, like goodness, was indefinable, something you knew when you experienced it. He found nearing seventy, he was able to put more of himself into his work and as a result it felt more satisfying than at any time of his career. A woman colleague, Iris Hudson from the drama department, had encouraged his more subjective efforts that surprisingly for him found a receptive audience in some good journals. He got the impression that his inclinations were being more broadly felt. Caspar drew on historical sources, and current works such as the recent book by a French scholar on the philosophy of walking and a book on Titian undertaken more as the author's journey of discovery than a standard art history tome, to help give shape to his own more narrative efforts. This is not to say, thought Caspar, that one should not make every effort for clarity and lucidity in thinking and writing. It's just that he wanted philosophy, particularly aesthetics, to be more related to art and life.

He found that his own work in photography educated him about aesthetics and creativity in ways that books alone could not. And it kept him humble. Making art was difficult. There was no formula. But it could also be divinely rewarding in rare moments. Talking in arcane and clever ways about art was no guarantee that someone could engage in any given case with true feeling and understanding. And this applied in ethics as well.

In the bedroom closet he took out his white oxford shirt, black chinos, black vee neck sweater, green socks, brown shoes, and grey tweed jacket. He tended to wear out a few items steadily liking the way clothes felt that had assumed the shape of his body. He travelled down West 4th Avenue on the bus downtown to the university. He couldn't help noticing all the Adsett's Realty signs on properties for sale.

# 2

The class was waiting. Veronica Ip was Caspar's PhD student from the National Institute of Fine Arts, Guangzhou, China, where he was a visiting professor. At twenty-five she had completed her master's in Classical Chinese Art and Philosophy and was beginning her third year of the aesthetics program. She had told Caspar quite definitely on first meeting him that she wanted him to call her "Veronica." She was aiming to write a thesis on the aesthetics of loss in traditional communities created by the destruction of ancient homes and temples in China, a thesis she could not write at home. She wanted to do it but was afraid to do it at the same time.

Veronica was diminutive. At around five foot two and very slim she had beautiful brown eyes, long black hair and flawlessly smooth almost creamy skin. She dressed usually in a short black leather jacket worn over a red cashmere sweater, narrow black jeans over black boots, and a trace of cinnamon eye shadow and dark lipstick. She was extremely intelligent, well-prepared, conceptually precise, and able to bring her own cultural and imaginative slant on issues. On being asked one day how she would define happiness she had replied in her fluent English, "Oh, but we wouldn't, it would be far too limiting."

Despite his many invitations she would not or could not call him Caspar. It was always, "professor," or "Dr. Ballantyne." On one occasion he had brought her an article from the Globe and Mail about Tiananmen Square. She had recoiled as if scalded and covered her eyes. Later she said to him quietly, "Professor you must realize every Chinese lives with fear in their heart." In his private self he found her heart-stoppingly beautiful.

Cy Russell, Caspar's other PhD student now in his third year also and around the same age as Veronica, came from the Nicola

Valley in British Columbia, an area of rolling grasslands, mountains and forest eight or nine hundred metres above sea level and a four-hour drive east of Vancouver. His parents owned a working cattle ranch off the old road from Merritt to Kamloops. In his high school days Cy had competed on the rodeo circuit. He was a tall and robust looking guy, with his left shoulder slightly lower than his right due to a meeting with a bull. He always wore his cowboy boots, faded blue jeans and tee shirts under a battered brown leather jacket. He was sometimes seen walking across campus in his cowboy hat, not for him an affectation but a longstanding part of his life. Cy had a gift for academic work and a passion for philosophy. His interest was in the aesthetics of the ranch and cowboy life. He was aiming to put some conversations and photographs in his thesis. What would qualify his study as a doctorate was a question much discussed in tutorial meetings.

There were three other students in the class, all female, who were taking the course as an option. For a few sessions the class would be discussing Kant's Critique of Judgement published in 1790. Although much criticized due to its supposed lack of social relevance, Caspar felt that it nevertheless remained the cornerstone of western aesthetics. He had loved Kant's view of the primary role of feeling and the mind's free play, not concepts, in judging beauty -- free beauty as he called it -- such that an aesthetic judgment had to be singular. In such a case, you couldn't reason your way to a judgment that something was beautiful. A painting such as a portrait was under a concept, however, but even so in apprehending an original work there could be no rule for balancing feeling and reason giving art an unfathomable elusiveness. Kant's aesthetics was really a kind of alchemy. This material would take more than one class to cover and argue about. He loved the story of Wittgenstein having the ceilings raised by an inch in the house he had designed for his sister, so they felt right to him. Caspar remembered the Critique being given short shrift by some at Cambridge, who laughingly referred to it as "continental dribble." The work might be a strange metaphysics in today's eyes but as an understanding of aesthetic experience it was still, for Caspar, unmatched. From being an unmentionable topic in philosophy, beauty was now back on the radar, given the plethora of recent books and articles on the subject.

Whatever, Caspar knew he couldn't exist without some beauty in his life, which for him gave substance to more ultimate and intrinsic values. What after all, was life for, all the striving and accumulation? Surely one could be moral, have a concern for others, and work for money without losing sight of the qualities of a leaf or drawing, and a myriad of things in daily life, each having its own unique value for mind and heart. Indeed, without moments of appreciation what was there to be loved and protected? Caspar knew he was fortunate in his work and life. People had to survive; it wasn't easy. But some core of value had to be maintained beyond the reach of the market.

# 3

Later that afternoon Caspar received an email from Dr. Neha Coomarasamy, his friend and colleague and professor of logic, asking him to come to her place for Christmas lunch, which was by now ten days away. Oh hell, he thought immediately. He liked Neha, she was about his age, maybe a bit younger, and he had over time felt many affinities with her. Growing up in Sri Lanka she had come to Canada with her family in her teens a product of a girls' boarding school. She was a well-established scholar, full prof, and an excellent teacher. She was tough intellectually, highly respected, had been the department chair, and was considered a great thesis advisor. She was always very warmly disposed to Caspar, their having achieved a trusting platonic intimacy rare in academic circles. Yet he fought shy of the invitation. After all these years he felt a bit scared at the prospect of being seriously alone with her and honestly he was getting used to the solitary life. So he answered "Dear Neha, thank you but I think I'll have a quiet day at home." The answer came back immediately, "For fuck's sake Cas, it's just lunch. Please come." So, somewhat warily he said he would.

The fall term came to an end. Caspar was marking essays, getting grades in. On Christmas Day he set off in the Buick, for an apartment in Point Grey. A sprinkling of fresh snow decorated the trees and streets. Neha welcomed him in with a hug. She was dressed in a short-sleeved, pale grey, cashmere figure hugging dress opened in a modest vee at the neck and sitting just below the knee. Around her neck was a double string of freshwater pearls, a silver Haida bracelet on her left wrist, silver stockings and on her feet a pair of shiny red shoes. Her long black hair, streaked now with grey, was fashioned in a chignon. She had the build of a fifties film star. She looked stunning. Her light brown skin reverberated against everything she was wearing. He handed her a bottle of chilled white wine. She led him into the kitchen, which was warm and filled with rich cooking aromas. "It won't be long. Take off your jacket and have a drink and get one for me."

He'd been here often over the years with Marjorie but this was kind of different. He was getting the feel of it. The wine relaxed him. He refilled his glass. The table was set with a white linen cloth, a vase of purple lisianthus blooms, and a pair of silver candlesticks with lit white candles.

So, Cas how are you? I hardly ever see you."

"Oh, I'm ok I guess," he said. "I still find myself talking to her and I dream a lot."

Neha came over and put her hand on his shoulder. "It takes time you know." Neha's husband, a biology professor, had decamped five years ago with a female graduate student, a not unheard of phenomenon in university circles. The older prof, married, being drawn to the adoring grad student or so it can seem in the beginning. Caspar sat in silence, just absorbing his surroundings, the situation, and Neha's perfume, which seemed to exude a smoky yet delicate sandalwood scent. He felt her closeness, her physical self, not by any means the scholar of logic. Then she moved away to attend to the lunch. Turning his head he looked at her, the way the dress moved over her shapely hips. He felt a tremor of something visceral stirring in him.

He sat quietly, savoring his drink, listening to Neha humming as she worked at the stove and counter. Then she turned and asked him to carve the turkey. She handed him a long, thin and narrow knife dark and stained, probably old carbon steel and a sharpening stone. Caspar put an edge on the knife then he was slicing meat, scooping out sage and onion stuffing from the inside and putting everything on a white china serving dish. "Ok Cas, two minutes," called out Neha. A moment later she was putting a dish of carrots and sprouts on the table, one of roast potatoes, a dish of cranberries, a gravy boat and the meat dish.

Sitting together they toasted each other a "Merry Christmas" and tucked into the dinner.

They took a little break after the savoury course, did some cleaning up then Neha asked Caspar to come back to the table. To his surprise she served a flaming Christmas pudding and brandy sauce adorned with a sprig of holly.

"I don't believe this," said Caspar, "Christmas pudding! I never knew this was an Indian tradition."

"Well, it isn't," said Neha. "I had it sometimes as a girl and thought you might like it."

"Well, I do, very much."

They took their coffee in the sitting room and sat chatting, relaxing, digesting the lunch. Neha put on some soft saxophone music. Caspar felt suffused with the warmth of friendship and dinner. Around four o'clock, Caspar asked Neha if she would like some help clearing up. She told him thanks but she would take care of it. So he stood up making motions to go. She fetched his coat. At the door they stood for a moment. Caspar said, "Thank you so much Neha. The meal was lovely and the company…" At that point she leaned into him, her face straining to meet his, and kissed him gently on the lips, the kiss lasting just a bit longer than usual among friends. He stood for a moment looking down into her eyes before returning the gesture, holding her by her shoulders.

"See you soon," said Caspar pulling away. With that he left, his feelings taking in what has just transpired between them. If anything he had wanted to embrace her more fully, feel her body against him. One thing about Neha, she might be a logician but she was incredibly in her body and he liked her spirit, always had. The visit, so enjoyable, had made him realize he'd been living a rather stunted life.

Neha stood by the door for a few moments wondering herself what had passed between them.

In the days that followed Caspar tried to put Christmas day out of his mind, give his emotions a chance to settle. Yet he couldn't stop imagining being with Neha again, absorbing her hypnotic perfume, noticing so many things about her, about her way of being a woman. She had intrigued and moved him, so different somehow, from Marjorie -- a thought he tried to quell the moment it arose. Marjorie was who she was and he had loved her for it. He told himself to get a grip, nothing had really happened.

# 4

The January semester was underway; a research semester for Caspar meaning no teaching. A time to write, go to China for a week or so, attend a philosophy conference, and without trying too hard find inspiration. In these later years, he felt the need to break out of the goal-driven, techno-marketing zeitgeist: the endless emails, smart phone intrusions, and media shit and express himself. What he wanted was voice, that true and distinctive ring of the individual self. These days this attitude and the critical view that goes with it was likely to be seen as a mark of resistance, being an awkward bastard, making people feel uncomfortable, not socially responsible, resistant to corporate goals, the strategic plan, not being a team player. No, Caspar thought, I'm not going to play that compliance game. He didn't want to upset people but that could not rule out the critical examination of ideas in favour of group think.

Caspar met with Neha mid-January having invited her to dinner at a little local restaurant in a small town on the Fraser River estuary. The restaurant was in what had once been a fishing and small boat repair building with wooden boards covering interior walls and ceiling painted white but yellowed with age. The tables and chairs were quite eclectic in shape and size gathered together over the years. All the tables had on them white cloths with place settings, green napkins, dim lights with small vases of assorted flowers. There was no menu, usually just a choice of two main courses one of which was always fish. Frank the owner and chef, a grizzled guy wearing a red-checked shirt and jeans with a white apron tied around the waist, smiled and said, "Hello professor, long time no see."

"Yes," Caspar said, you're right. Frank I'd like you to meet my friend Neha Coomarasamy." Frank looked back at Caspar unknowing, then at Neha, smiling.

"Frank," said Neha quietly, "Marjorie has passed away."

"Oh, I'm sorry professor, she was such a lovely person." At that he rested his hand on Caspar's shoulder. Caspar nodded, agreeing with him, silently thanking him.

Then Frank stood for a moment before telling them what was available that evening. They opted for fresh steamed halibut with prunes in a white parsley sauce that hinted of lavender with green beans, and a bottle of BC Gerwertztraminer. Neha looked around and said the place was charming and wondered how she had never known about it. They had chatted all evening about nothing significant, enjoying the wine and the moment. Each privately marveling at the fact they were even alone together like this.

They met a week or so later at the old seaplane base café by Jericho beach. It was too cold for the balcony outside but they liked the plain diner type room inside and the unstuffy menu and atmosphere. Sitting down they caught a faint whiff of a joint. Maybe it was this leftover feeling from the hippie Kitsilano sixties that prompted them to take a further step. Almost at the same moment they each started to ask whether the other would like to come back for a nightcap. They arrived back at Neha's around nine. A cold winter's night. She made coffee and poured a couple of brandies. They talked for a while, then both went quiet. Caspar put down his coffee cup and stood up. Moving over to her he kissed her on her cheek. Neha stood up, clasped her arms around his neck and kissed him as he pulled her to into him and pressed his lips onto hers breathing in her hypnotic aroma. She responded kissing him with parted lips and more ardour. "Cas, Cas, how I've longed to do that." He looked, mesmerized, into her shining brown eyes.

She clasped his hand and led him into her bedroom that had a low queen-sized bed and an Indian rug. She had draped a string of tiny blue lights, now lit, across the wall above the bed giving the room a sensory glow. On the creamy walls were some photographs and pictures that Caspar was not at this moment taking in. She lit an incense stick that wafted into his nostrils like an aromatic caress. They moved closer to the bed, which was covered with a terra cotta duvet, Caspar felt himself becoming unsteady. This was a whole new thing for him. He dropped down and lay back, not moving, just askew on the bed, his eyes closed. Neha sat on the bed, leaned over him, took his hand and said, "Caspar, it's just me, relax, we don't have to do anything."

"Neha," he whispered.

"Yes Cas," she answered, her tongue touching his ear.

"Are you sure about this?"

Neha kissed him and said, "Oh yes, very sure."

Caspar felt himself stirring. They undressed and lay down. He saw her in her full naked beauty, her lovely skin and hair the dark areolas of her nipples and her fulsome body and reached over and caressed her breast, before running his hand down her side onto her thigh. Neha sighed, and pulled him to her and kissing him ardently before saying "Cas, I love your fur," as she rubbed her hand over his chest. Caspar lay back. He seemed unsure of himself. She touched his face and said, "Cas, it's ok let yourself go." As they got together Caspar quite quickly reached his climax feeling orgasmic pleasure along with some pain from behind his scrotum. But all too quick for Neha. They both lay back, panting. "Neha, I…"

Neha whispered in his ear, "It's ok Cas, maybe we need more practice?" said as she smiled. She kissed him again on the lips, stroking his face.

Neha went into the bathroom and came out after a couple of minutes wearing a black silk kimono. "Let's have a drink," she said, passing Caspar a man's robe. He went into the bathroom and saw his flushed face in the mirror. Looking down he removed the condom, something he hadn't worn for years, and cleaned himself up. He washed his face and took a few deep breaths. Neha was the only woman he'd had sex with besides Marjorie in several decades. He didn't know how he'd managed it he was so nervous and in a sense, feeling he was in forbidden territory except that he could feel Neha's warmth of feeling towards him and she had such a carefree erotic presence. In the kitchen she produced some cigarettes, American, and they lit up filling the room with the rich smell of Turkish tobacco. They sat drinking scotch, smiling, watching the smoke swirl around the table.

# 5

By early February, Caspar had decided to go and work for a month in what was, had been, Marjorie's and his cottage on Lake Okanagan. He had not seen Neha for a couple of weeks, though they had spoken on email of getting together. Neha telling him she was missing him and sending kisses. If it hadn't been for his sense of time running on the meter he might not have invited her, for the invitation was a shift in his view of who he was now and where he was headed. On the one hand he was beginning to like coming home to an empty apartment. He could just get a drink, fill his pipe and get on with it from the old leather chair. Given his work, the needs of his students, and his various interests, he was not feeling especially lonely. Also, somewhat guiltily, he was quite liking the lack of complication in his life: the compromises, negotiations, and upsets that came from being married.

And yet, he wanted more of her, her company and yes by all means her body, her scent, her skin, her responsiveness, her taste, and unabashed sexuality. As Caspar was now being reminded, it was marvelous to love and share each other's erotic energies. So not surprisingly Caspar invited her to come out to the cottage for a few days. She replied next day to say she would love to come. As he read her email he thought ye gods! From somewhere deep in his psyche there was a bit of a nervous ripple. For Caspar had not, understandably, begun to consider what it might mean to be in a relationship with a woman like Neha. A woman who took to life with a great deal of vital appetite and confidence. And Caspar had by comparison been leading a pretty conservative kind of life. And not forgetting the matter of age, his own physical capabilities, and his remaining attachment to Marjorie's memory, could such a relationship even be possible? And yet he couldn't help noticing a rise in his spirits.

So Saturday morning, early February he was motoring along heading east on highway 1. He turned on the radio and heard the Beatles playing "Here Comes the Sun." He loved that one. Some student had played it regularly in his university drawing class, which back then was focused entirely on the nude. Then straight after was George Harrison's "While My Guitar Gently Weeps." Oh, things were looking up as he hummed along. At fifty miles out the first sign of mountains were shadowing the fertile Fraser valley. Coming through Hope and on the road through Manning Park, snow covered peaks were all around. Little traffic. A long drive came next through the mountains stopping at Princeton for coffee. The Buick, purring along, twenty years old and still going strong. An hour later, passing through Keremeos, a small fruit-growing village where Marjorie had always bought peaches and apricots for canning. The terrain was drier now, going through sandy, pine covered mountains. Then into Penticton on the southern tip of Lake Okanagan, and onto the road to Naramata. Naramata, a one-time fruit growing village and district, on the lake's edge now given over to vineyards and the up-market culture that goes with it.

After half an hour Caspar drove through a gate a couple of miles before the village. A winding mountain road carried on for a few miles up to the base of a lightly forested sandstone massif populated by black bears, deer, cougars, eagles, and rattlesnakes. Caspar drove onto a graveled track that twisted its way down through trees and steep, wind–buffeted sandy bluffs, over a little bridge and creek, until the road opened out onto a wider grassy area with the cottage tucked into cottonwood trees by the lakeshore. He parked by the porch steps, went in and unpacked taking a look in each room, switching on the power. Logs were stacked ready by the woodstove. He had come here alone many times in the past to work and also to give Marjorie some space.

He found it therapeutic to immerse himself in his own thoughts from time to time.

The cottage was built in 1911 with fir floors, cedar siding, a shake roof, and white plaster walls. There was one large room with a sitting area and kitchen, a bedroom and bathroom. Nothing fancy. He looked at the bed and thought of Neha in it.

He put stuff away and slipped on his down vest and toque. Outside it was cold, around freezing, the sky clear. He stood for a while taking it in, the quiet, the air, the sounds of the trees and water. The ice-encrusted creek bubbling close by. Then the strange strangled gurgle sound of a raven. There were a few of them resident in the gully but he couldn't see anything. He set off and took a walk on a path by the beach. The lake he knew of old running roughly north and south, seventy-five miles long, three or so miles wide and very deep. For many years he had loved getting into the lake for swimming for the sheer experience of being submerged, cut off from the clamour of the world. Feeling the water on his skin, smelling it, diving down among the shards of light fading into the greeny depths, naked: a glorious feeling. Down here in the ravine he was cut off from the main road or neighbours. Passing canoeists were not bothered by him. His body was ready to go in, but not at this temperature.

Along the bench, under the mountains, most of the old orchards had been cut down. Little was left of the earlier fruit-growing life and economy and for Caspar this was a cause for lament. The rambling processing plant had been downed, the railway line taken up. For some weeks in the summer Marjorie and he would seek out an old guy, Bill Blake, selling fruit, eggs and cabbages. A holdout. He seemed at peace with the world. His black Pomeranian, "Bear," always by his side.

Getting colder now, a thin layer of snow on the ground, ice at the water's edge. Time to get inside. Make a fire. He got the wine out of the fridge. A bottle of local Chardonnay. Then he made himself a cheese and chutney sandwich and poured a glass. Quebec cheddar, Marjorie's favourite and the last of her plum chutney. He stood there leaning against the battered Formica counter, just listening, voices and conversations. She was with him now wearing a beach wrap around her swimsuit. He was for a moment, about to take her a glass of wine on the veranda where she was sitting reading shaded by the roof overhang.

She knew his fault lines and strengths. She always drove the car knowing how much he liked to keep a keen eye on the landscape. How often had they sat in the kitchen at home as he related some problem from work. She was such a rock. Cleverer than him he knew. Helping him through his medical emergencies. Strange, how he felt her nearer to him in the cottage. After a while he put on the light, took his sandwich to the table bringing with him his book, some young academic writing about hiking the historic footpaths of Britain. No doubt about it walking was in. Afterwards he got up, filled his pipe, and remembering lit it inside.

Next morning, out of bed, making tea, dark and strong. He had several big mugsful with sugar. Breakfast was oatmeal, bacon and eggs, toast with dark chunky marmalade. Later, he drove up past the village for a stretch before turning onto the steep switchback road leading up the mountain to the railway line. It was cold and snowing lightly. He parked, pulled out his backpack and hiking poles, and headed up the railway track noting the signs warning of rattlesnakes.

Rising gradually, heading up the valley, mountains all around. Looking south towards Penticton he could see the swathe of vineyards clearly delineated, zigzagging in all directions. He kept going until he crossed over a semi-frozen creek that gushed under the path down to the lake. Just past to the right was a hiking trail that headed up into the high snowbound mountains.

At this point he drank some water and fixed up his camera around his neck. He set off up the trail going through the trees, mostly ponderosa pine with occasional Douglas fir, some cedar, aspen, birch and juniper. He broke through the snow stopping to look through the camera's viewfinder. It was quiet and still. Bears and snakes would be in hibernation. There could be the odd cougar about, and possibly some great grey owls, ospreys, red-tailed hawks, deer and of course, ravens. He scanned the area, adjusting the filter and took a shot looking up the trail into the trees, snow untouched.

Higher up the trail he noted a possible eagle or osprey perch on a large pine. At the foot of the tree he saw small bones, sculls, beaks, bones from larger animals, feet and feathers. He took a picture looking up the trail. He remembered a fashion photographer saying recently what's the point of photographing trees? A tree is just a tree. How wrong can you be? Each tree is distinct, the product of its history, weather, luck in its position, type and much else.

Caspar loved trees. He took many photographs of them appreciating their uniqueness as living entities. And streams. He loved getting into the cool flowing water, lying on the streambed feeling the rush of water over him in the light and perfume of air. It was for him a kind of intoxication. After about an hour on the trail he headed back. In the days that followed he started each day with a two-hour hike then returned to the cottage to sit and think, read, write notes, look through his photographs and have a glass of wine.

He was ruminating on the idea of writing something on landscape and photography. And for Caspar, appreciation was his talisman, for him an aim of life. He was just roaming around in his thoughts at the moment. He kept a small journal of field notes with him and made observations on his walks: on nature, philosophy, and other random things he could think about. He had taken to heart what Wittgenstein had said about his own investigations about language, which he described as sketches of landscapes made in the course of long and complicated journeys. And his notion, whether he meant it literally or not, that philosophy should only be written as poetry. In his writing Wittgenstein used numbered notes that cycled ideas around for reconsideration, more of a collage than anything else. There was no wonder Caspar and others found him sympathetic--the man himself was an artist.

When he could, he would set off from the apartment in a looping route across fifty or sixty city blocks noting things of interest, occasionally taking pictures, or getting into conversations about for example a flicker on the sidewalk or a vintage home. But mostly on these walks he would disappear into himself just being in the rhythm of walking and breathing not conscious of the physical effort involved. When spoken to he did not often respond being unaware of others. In the cottage that week he continued his hikes with afternoons and evenings devoted to academic work having faith that something would emerge. He never worked with a definite plan just an approximate sense of direction.

# 6

This being Saturday morning he was waiting at the arrivals gate at Penticton airport. He was meeting Neha on the ten o'clock flight from Vancouver. She came out looking composed and chic and waved as she saw him. She had on jeans and a light orange down jacket. They hugged and he picked up her suitcase asking her if she had been to Penticton before. She had not. In the car now on the road to Naramata running through the benchlands and vineyards overlooking the lake.

"But Cas," she exclaimed, "this is so amazing" and then no words, just looking. Going through the gate and dropping down through the winding sandy gulley she was amazed at the wildness of it all. He led her inside the cottage. "It's lovely Cas, thank you for asking me." She leaned into him and kissed him on the lips as he embraced her and kissed her back. Caspar said they could go for a walk and he took her up to the railway path where they walked up to an old tunnel taking in the views before returning.

He directed her to the bedroom, told her where she could put things, and showed her the bathroom. Then he left her to it for a while and went and made tea. Caspar looked at her as they sat chatting taking in her aura, and the strange fact she was here. A number of times she rested her hand over his forearm when relating some bit of faculty politics. They sat and drank looking out across the lake. "But enough of that," she said. "What I want to know is what are we eating?" She disappeared and came back with a bottle of wine and a bottle of single malt.

"Gad Neha, thank you but it's too much. So kind of you." She smiled.

"Well then, would you like a glass of wine while I make the pasta? You can talk to me."

"For sure, go to it" she replied.

Neha lit a cigarette. The aroma made him stop for a second.

Caspar started a tomato sauce to have with penne and parmesan, and a little salad to follow. Quite soon he put on the pasta pot to boil. And ten minutes later dropped in the penne. Neha topped up his glass. "I never realized Cas, you're pretty good at this." They ate. She asked about the cottage and the area. It was getting dark. A candle was burning on the table. He made coffee, put out some lemon cake from the village shop, and poured each of them a finger of Neha's scotch. "Well thank you Caspar, that was all yummy." At ten, Neha said yawning, "Maybe we should clean up. It's my bedtime."

"I'll clean up," said Caspar, "you just go. You have the blue towels."

Caspar had almost done when he heard her shout, "I'm out."

When he opened the bedroom door twenty minutes later she didn't move. He got in and lay still. Steady breathing from Neha, her head barely visible under the duvet. Caspar slid down and turned on his side. A chance this weekend, he thought, to be in each other's company--discover things about each other even as they were sharing this playing field of a bed.

Odd, but he had always slept best in this room. It was pretty basic. Of course, there was the whole rich history of the cottage. For a few moments he had the disconcerting feeling that Neha was actually an interloper. How difficult it is to take on the whole physical and psychological reality of another human being. No banish the thought. Time to be bold. He could hear nothing but the wind in the trees and the gurgling of the creek right outside.

Opening his eyes he looked over his shoulder and saw that Neha was out of bed. Listening, he made out the sounds of the shower. Then, "Caspar could you come in here please?" He opened the door to light and steam. Morning sun was streaming in. "Neha was in the shower silhouetted through the plastic curtain. She pulled it back and looked at him standing in his boxers, saying, "Come on Cas get in."

He didn't move for a moment then pulled off his boxers and climbed in. She was of course all wet, soapy, and very naked. She reached out and soaped his chest pulling him closer and said "Good morning."

"Good morning Neha."

They pressed up against each other for a moment, the sun glinting off her hair and shoulders. Caspar leaned back and looked down on her lovely body. He caressed and kissed her in the spray of the hot water. Neha turned around with her back to him holding onto the shower pipe. Caspar was not hesitant today. He wrapped an arm around her midriff and pushed into her, kissing her neck. It was physically exquisite for them both. After, Neha turned and looked into his eyes, touched his cheek and kissed him, smiling in the sunlight. They held onto each other until Caspar stepped out.

After a few minutes, Neha came into the kitchen wearing the black kimono, combing out her wet hair as Caspar handed her a mug of black coffee. "Smells good," she said, exuding a quality that could not be put into words, but which for Caspar was uniquely magical.

Alone again in the cottage, his senses still resonating with Neha, her scent lingering, he didn't want to change the sheets. He felt better than he had for an age.

# 7

Sitting with his books and notes one evening Caspar, musing about grad supervision, reflected he had told his students to resist the urge to bring dissertations to a too early completion. Mostly this means redoing the whole thing. Study, think, give things a chance to emerge. There is no recipe in philosophy. It's a form of literature. But he gave them his guidelines: Five chapters, one hundred and fifty pages to be completed in one to two years. Be modest with your bibliography. Excess in referencing is for the social sciences, it also betrays a trust in publication that may be unwarranted. Avoid talk of behaviour. He remembered the old joke: Two behavioural psychologists had finished making love. One of them says to the other, "Well, that was good for you how was it for me?" People had minds, webs of personal history and inclination, feeling, a taste for irony, a capacity for understanding and creativity, ghosts in the machine if you like. No one could really explain it no matter how scientifically it was dressed up. Better to live with some mystery than fall prey to facile speculations. Respect the literature but you are the critical architect of the work. This is what makes for a doctorate.

There was an art in thesis writing; all writing, a required element of voice and style and this was the hardest thing to teach. Now older and wiser he knew that at heart everything was subjective even as we struggle for truth. Having supervised more than twenty doctoral theses he had a good sense of what was required, of what external examiners would be looking for. Aesthetic arguments were persuasive rather than given as proofs, but persuasion of a very high order with moments of originality woven into a coherent and well-expressed whole. A thesis in aesthetics could have its own aesthetic character.

For Caspar the arts came closest to providing authentic expressions of what it meant to be human. He liked the words of one nineteenth-century French writer, Emile Zola, who thought of art as a little fragment of the world seen through a temperament.

Much contemporary art, especially that which required obscure theoretical knowledge in order to understand it, was not for him. Yet he had appreciated a line made by walking in a field as done by one conceptual artist, and he liked much abstract art. It was a free country. People could do what they liked. He couldn't play the old philosophical game of defining art though. He was not about to legislate. If a load of bricks could be art etc. Caspar had honed his preferences. What he wanted for himself was an art produced by skill and imagination.

Philosophy, he thought, could be a close second to art in exploring human life provided it did not get too caught up with verbal jousting and analysis. Moral philosophy for him was not simply about the logic of moral argument or formulas such as utilitarianism, though he did have some time for the categorical imperative. For Caspar there had to be a place in ethics for love and goodness. It took a woman philosopher, Iris Murdoch, who was also an artist, to remind scholars of this.

He had completed the piece of photography and landscape and sent it to an aesthetics journal.

# 8

Back in Vancouver, Caspar asked Veronica and Cy individually to meet with him and each bring along a thesis proposal. He told them their study had to be doable in a year.

Cy was proposing a study of the aesthetics of his parents' cattle ranch, including a critical analysis of its history, crafts, culture and working life, its impact on the indigenous people of the Nicola Valley, plants, wild creatures, and the animals of the ranch. He would write passages of narrative and include photographs and drawings. Veronica wanted to go ahead with a study of the aesthetics of loss of the ancient architecture of Guangzhou. Caspar knew from his own work at the Art Institute that this could upset people who were intent on moving as fast as possible on the project of modernization and development. Also not forgetting there was no room for criticism, direct or implied, of the government in China. But that had to be balanced in Canada against the principle of academic freedom and the production of a worthy study. Veronica had come to Canada specifically to work on the idea. Caspar asked her to let him think about it and they would meet again in a couple of days.

For Caspar, city walking was a kind of fieldwork, filling out his more abstract world with the living, changing, buzz of life. For him the aesthetic was an essential part of his responsive repertoire. Appreciation, he believed could reasonably foster preservation. There were limits to this scheme for Caspar, however. That which is evil, he thought, could not be beautiful. Photographs of hooded ku klux clan members, for example, or Nazis in their regalia, thought by some to be beautiful, could never be in Caspar's mind, not when you considered what these people represented. He would never show such photographs in his class being unwilling to spread their poison. For him beauty was an image of the good. Many disagreed with him about that, nevertheless, in such cases he was critically undaunted. He walked to calm his nerves, take the air, smell the scents, be in the world, and keep the blood flowing. He was still having some prostate pain but it seemed manageable as long as he followed doctor's orders. It was mid-March, and Vancouver was well into its spring. Cherry blossoms were out, fresh new green leaves were sprouting on bushes and trees, camellia and magnolia flowers were blooming, early rhododendrons were splashing colour, and forest-like canopies were gaining their cover on the long avenues running thirty or so blocks west to Alma from Granville Street. Large, impressive trees of many varieties lined the streets thanks to the foresight of the early city planners and horticulturalists. Out on Jericho and Spanish Banks, the long stretches of open grass, trees and beaches by English Bay, he appreciated all the new growth, and the wild nature of the park. He carried his tree book, bird book, small binoculars, camera, notebook, water, and backpack as always.

Crossing Spanish Banks Creek, a Coho salmon stream, he headed up the path alongside the northern boundary of Spirit Park with large trees of many species covering a high bank on his left. Across the water looking northwest, and in the distance up Howe Sound, snow-capped peaks ranged impressively in the spring light. One mountain, diamond-shaped at its peak, stood out from the rest, towering, and sublime. Herons, seagulls, eagles, song sparrows, red-winged blackbirds, chickadees, and crows were all around. He watched a bald eagle circling and rising on a current of warm air over the water, wings outstretched seemingly making no effort. Canada geese were honking after each other. On his previous walk he had spotted a whale spout in the Bay followed by a breach and lifting of flukes. Two herons flapped by overhead looking like long lost DC 3s. Incredible. He reminded himself that come summer he would be out there swimming. The sky was cloudless, with some slight haze and the light was edging towards the golden, yet a cool wind still buffeted him as he walked.

He walked as far as a little memorial of flowers encased in an upturned log and turned around stopping off for a tea and a sit at the concession. He and Marjorie had done this walk together countless times. There were constant reminders of her presence as he strode along. She would be telling him the latest escapades and challenges of kids in her classes. Particular individuals she had a soft spot for usually bad characters, so to speak, kids from straitened circumstances, like her own had been.

She gave out a lot for them. She took her classes on field trips often over weekends and sponsored the History Club. She told them about Tommy Douglas, one time premier of Saskatchewan, who organized the first public health care system in Canada. He was one of her heroes. But also she had kept in close touch with her parents helping them out financially and moving them into a little house on the edge of the Derbyshire countryside where they spent their retirement.

Caspar stopped off at the washroom, more needed of late, and set off for the trek back up to Kits. He loved the wildness of Vancouver, so much for his eye to take in, to identify, hear and smell. On a recent day, walking over Burrard Bridge, a bald eagle had suddenly risen up above the guardrail on his right-hand side only feet away from him lingering for a moment. He froze. Then the big creature was off. First Nations people, having their own rich culture, and living by the ocean and in the forests for thousands of years had managed to live sublimely in harmony with nature. Caspar realized he reaped the benefit of this stewardship.

More than anything he loved seeing ravens on his city walks. He knew of a nest under the Granville Street Bridge. They were large and wild. Their lovely blue black streamlined heads and beaks and glossy feathers. They had an incredible wingspan. The crows got upset when ravens settled on branches in their territory and would dive-bomb them noisily until they left. Crows in Vancouver could be quite ferocious. They nested in the trees on his street and would buzz him on leaving the apartment. At egg laying and chick rearing times he would leave with an umbrella unfurled as protection. These smart little gangsters knew how to draw blood from passers by.

# 9

Neha. Neha in herself was, or had been, undergoing something of a transformation. She was for one thing more involved in her career than ever, working at it with gusto. Not wanting to waste a moment. There were books to be written. She had always enjoyed her field, but now she would work through the night, any time of day, whenever the mood took her. In demand academically, she accepted numerous speaking engagements around the world. After her husband had left, she had at first been quite miserable. It had taken her a while to get over it. Fortunately, he worked at the other university. Then, far from being the unhappy deserted wife she had made the discovery that her new life suited her, academically and personally. She'd had intimate encounters with a number of men varying in age. The split from her husband had enabled her to follow her own inclinations, not in any organized way, she let the world come to her, nothing forced, no casting around on the web.

She developed a friendship with a woman painter named Deirdre or Dee, who lived on the East Side in a bit of a ramshackle turn of the century four story building divided up into artists' spaces with living accommodation. They had met at a gallery opening in Gastown and quickly developed a relationship. Dee was a woman of Scottish origins from Nova Scotia who had been to the art school there a couple of decades earlier. She was seriously into her painting and worked at a grocery store part-time. She frequented the local heavy metal music scene, had a number of piercings and tattoos, and liked to wear tight black leggings, boots, costume jewelry, and had extravagantly coloured hair.

Neha, to her own surprise, had loved their encounters, being with someone so different, a free-thinker, un-academic. She admired Dee's butterfly tattoo on the inside curve of her right breast, her shoe collection, tight skirts, long snug tee shirts. She loved their talks about life and men, and loved the cooking and eating at Dee's Aladdin's cave of an apartment, taking up showering together and the occasional sleepover, which after her long marriage was a revelation. She surprised herself, felt a luxurious letting go. Their relationship eased off to something more platonic after a few months due to each other's busy lives, but also because as it turned out, Dee was prolific in her circle of acquaintances.

The younger guys she met were exciting at first, in their youth and sinewy beauty and, amazingly, their passion for her as an older woman. But she couldn't talk with them, if that mattered. Who she was or who she was to be in this stage of her life was undecided. She was with relish winging it. She had always been a good dresser, but now she indulged her love of clothes, and lingerie. She hadn't gone in for this with Caspar so far, for some reason, perhaps because there was still something of the forbidden about him. He had surprised her though with his passion and she could definitely talk to him.

Ah Caspar, Caspar, how to explain chemistry? Here he was pushing seventy yet he had for her still a charisma that drew her to him, more so than any other. She liked him. She liked his way of being. He was fun and interesting to be with and very much present when with her, not constantly checking his damn cell phone, never in fact, or being distractedly in his own world. He looked her in the eye. And now after so many years they had finally made love and she had not been disappointed.

# 10

Veronica already had a stock of photographs and research on different cases of architectural destruction she had brought with her from Guangzhou. Caspar remembered on one of his visits to the Institute there asking his Chinese colleagues whether there were concerns about what he could only see as being irreplaceable cultural losses of ancient buildings. Their response surprised him. They told him that as China was a five thousand year old culture there was nothing to worry about and that in any case they felt they had a long way to go to catch up with the west in terms of modernization. He had done his best to sound a note of caution especially in regard to market economics; they didn't seem to understand the destructive power of the global market, but he felt nobody was in a mood to listen. People were getting consumer goods such as fridges and cars and they were travelling abroad, their children going to university in the west, the more educated, well-placed middle classes that is. Life was getting better if not for the migrant factory workers. The deal was though that there could be nothing resembling democracy. And now under the current president even stricter state suppression of civil liberties was in force. No one could safely speak out about anything.

Caspar asked Veronica in their follow up meeting whether she thought her project would be risky? She said maybe a little but she felt it was necessary. Her parents, she said, were supportive. They had been Red Guards and had been members of the Party for many years. She said she hoped to publish the thesis. Caspar was close to retirement. Any fallout from Veronica's work would be unlikely to affect him, but as her supervisor he felt responsible for her. Academically he would like the study to go ahead but he would not be taking much of a risk. His feeling safe made him feel weak somehow. It was backwards. He had asked himself would he like his daughter to be in Veronica's place? He knew he wouldn't. He asked himself if he was getting things out of proportion? And yet not to support her would be a form of self-censorship that could be a slippery slope. Yes, but he was supposed to have his students' best interests at heart. But what were they? Caspar asked her, "Do you not have any other possibilities? What about a similar study on architecture in Vancouver?" There were plenty of cases of homes being demolished to make way in old neighborhoods for oversized, alien and characterless houses. Couldn't she draw any parallels? He asked her, what if she could never go home after this work? What if she couldn't see her parents again? But he couldn't shift her.

Caspar had never before had to face such a situation. He was a professor in a Canadian university. Nobody ever bothered what his students did. But this was political. So was any philosophical position up to a point, but not like this. He knew he could just say, no sorry you will have to do something else. But he had always expected his students to come up with their own thesis ideas. It was part of being an independent thinker. And it gave them ownership. He said he needed a bit more time and would get in touch with a decision in a couple more days.

Later that day Caspar phoned his old colleague Dr. Ruth Yueng and asked to see her. Ruth had left China as a young student to study at McGill University and never went back. He told her in brief the situation and forwarded Veronica's proposal. The next morning they met in Ruth's office. Ruth was a professor in the history department with interests in Asian culture and philosophy. After their greetings Ruth said "So Caspar, you are getting involved in some real politik eh? If you want my opinion you have to go with it. Your student knows her situation better than you. My guess is that she would leave the university or find another prof if you say no. She has chosen you Caspar, don't imagine it's the other way around."

He sat quietly for a few moments, then said, "Ruth, would you be willing to be second member?"

"Yes, of course, if you want me."

"Well, I'd want you for sure."

"Sounds like you've made a decision, then."

"Yes, I'll approve the proposal and if its ok with you let her know you'll join us."

"By all means Caspar, delighted to be working with you again."

Caspar met with Veronica and told her she could go ahead. She was to make an appointment with Dr. Yeung to discuss her intentions and he would see to the paperwork. And that seemed to be that. She looked at him and said, "Thank you Professor Ballantyne. You are very kind. I will do my best." At that she stood up, bowed her head slightly in his direction and left the office.

For Cy, he wasn't sure about the second member. Cy's suggestion of a colleague in the philosophy department, a professor of language and mind, with whom Caspar had had a somewhat uneasy relationship gave him pause. Cy explained that he had worked well with this professor in a course and felt sure there was a sympathy for the philosophical direction and subject of the thesis. Professor Norbert Honeywell, a veteran of the department. Unmarried. A bit fussy and in Caspar's mind not the person you want on a thesis committee that challenges some of the norms of tradition.

He thought not. Politics unfortunately come into everything. He said he would think about it and in the meantime Cy was to get started. Really though it was a problem. Who could he ask who had the capacity and willingness to do the job and would be a good collegial committee member? But the first hurdle was the comprehensive exams, which qualified them to be PhD candidates able to write their theses. They took their papers after a month of preparation and both passed with no problems.

All seemed to be well until not long after Veronica came to see him with an email in Chinese, translated by her hand underneath, telling her to cease and desist work on her study. Caspar looked at her, this slight young woman, and said, "So Veronica, who do you think wrote this and how would they know what you are intending?"

"I don't know Professor, but there are many eyes even here. You have no idea. They keep watch on us. It's possible my computer has been hacked."

"This is incredible," said Caspar."

Veronica said nothing.

He looked at her. She was quite calm. She had grown up in a different world.

"Listen Veronica, I think I'd better discuss this with the President. You can carry on for now and I'll contact you as soon as I can. Try not to worry."

She thanked him, made a small bow and left.

"Fucking hell," thought Caspar. "This is a first."

# 11

He made an appointment to see the University President next day in the late afternoon telling the secretary it was an urgent and confidential matter, no agenda given. Caspar arrived on time and was ushered into the President's office.

The President, Dr. Shirley James, was a respected professor of archeology. She had grown up on a four-section grain farm in a small town in southern Saskatchewan. The town had six grain elevators, a short main street, a railway line, and a lit outdoor ice rink in winter. She was bused to a high school twenty miles away each day. Often not in winter if the temperature dipped below -20 degrees which it often did before global warming. After graduating with honours from the University of Saskatchewan in Saskatoon she went on to receive her doctorate from Harvard. Dr. James had had a distinguished career as a professor at Princeton before deciding it was time to come home. She was now in her mid-fifties, had silvery dark hair, was five foot ten, and had that prairie look, a bit gaunt but still handsome, and in the fourth year of her first five-year term. Liked mostly, as a straight shooter, she came in dressed in a grey business pantsuit and small purple Hermes scarf, shook Caspar's hand and said, "Well Cas, what's going on?" as he handed her the email.

"So this was received by your student?"

Caspar briefed her on the situation. Shirley sighed and said "Well it's funny, probably no connection, but I had a visit from the Secretary of the Pacific Rim Foundation, yesterday. They want to give us a grant of a million dollars to fund a new program of Asia Studies."

"Oh, that's nice. Why do I think there's a catch."

"Well not one that I know of, but you know there are always interests attached to these grants. Anyway, the Secretary said they were keen to see a program that would focus on Asian history and culture." Shirley switched on a small desk fan and lit a cigarette, offering one to Caspar who gratefully accepted even though they were now both breaking the no-smoking regulations.

"Look Cas, Harry Adsetts parlayed this grant. I know it's unorthodox for a Chancellor but who argues with a million dollars. Maybe we should be glad we've got him and we do need just such a program to address gaps in our curriculum. So he's got that right. But he also said, somewhat enigmatically, that we should ensure we all strive to maintain good relationships with our Pacific Rim friends. All said 'Hail fellow well met.' And of course I agreed with him. Anyway, sorry for the digression but tell me what your student's working on."

"Well, she wants to examine the cultural damage resulting from the demolition of ancient architecture in China by the real estate developers. I've discussed it with her, and suggested she focus on the situation in Vancouver, which is bad enough, but she's determined to stick to her idea." Caspar explained that he had consulted with Ruth Yueng and that she was of the opinion that the proposal should go ahead. "Actually we already gave Veronica our approval," he said, "even though the Chinese authorities won't like any public airing of cultural insensitivity on their part, as per the email."

These were upsetting thoughts for Caspar. He had enjoyed his time as a visiting professor in various art colleges over the years in China always receiving a warm welcome and great hospitality. He had enjoyed his teaching, and especially liked going into the studios running programs in classical landscape painting; the levels of skill and aesthetic sensitivity being shown speaking to years of discipline and commitment. He had felt great respect for the people there. He admired the Chinese spirit, the pragmatic, but also philosophical outlook formed by millennia of history, culture, and life. The Chinese knew who they were and loved their country. But they weren't fools either.

Shirley finished her cigarette, stubbed it out the said, "Cas, I will of course support you and Veronica. You might expect more problems. Who knows? This is unique in my experience." She sat quiet for a moment then started to say something else, stopped and shook her head slowly. What was she thinking Caspar wondered, but said nothing. Shirley looked directly at him, quivering slightly, "But you know, I don't actually have a lot of power and I can be undermined easily in the Senate on many issues. However, academic matters are the responsibility of Faculty, and my guess is the last thing the people who sent the email would want is for this to become a cause celebre. So for now do nothing. Just carry on as usual, but keep me informed."

Caspar was thinking ahead that he would have to choose the thesis examiners very carefully. He stood up, came around her desk and as she stood he shook her hand. "Thank you very much Shirley," he said, looking at her with feeling. "I'm grateful for your support."

She just looked back at him with a straight expression, flicking the ash from another cigarette into her desk drawer and said, "It's my job."

On the way out, it occurred to him that Shirley would soon have her own battles to fight as her re-appointment as President was coming up and had to be approved by the Board of Governors.

Caspar phoned Veronica to say she could go ahead with the University's approval.

He arrived home a day or two later to find his apartment door ajar, his desk drawers hanging open, papers on the floor, a chair overturned, nothing taken as far as he could see but very unsettling nonetheless. He immediately phoned the police who looked the place over, advised him to get a burglar alarm, take extra care locking up, and get in touch if anything else occurred. The next day, the phone rang at home with no number. There were a few clicks when he answered then a voice said, "Professor, you better give up this ridiculous work. Miss Li is Chinese citizen she must not go ahead with her project. And you Professor must be careful, you understand." With that more clicks and the line went dead, but definitely an English as a second language speaker. Bloody hell, are they really so sensitive, thought Caspar, afraid of a student's study. And now he too was to be threatened. It was insane.

As for Cy, Caspar had thought of someone who might do very nicely for his committee. Jeff Matthews was an indigenous assistant professor in Environmental and First Nations Studies at U of V, who had grown up in the Cariboo region, a high plateau in the interior of BC, and was familiar with cattle ranching, native life and local ecology. He had taken an honours philosophy degree at Toronto prior to doing his doctoral studies on ecology and the environment. Jeff complemented his case studies research with photographs, native storytelling and knowledge of the land. He proved to be a willing and indeed collegial committee member who had a great deal of personal knowledge and critical acumen to offer and Cy was happy with the choice. Caspar met with both students and their second members to make sure everyone was fully on board. He would be keeping his eye on things through regular contact and email.

# 12

Caspar decided at the beginning of the last week of his research semester that an evening phone call to Neha was overdue. Neha answered with a warm, "Hi Cas, so nice to hear from you. Sorry I haven't been in touch. You know, work. Would love to see you. Why not come over Saturday. We can order in. And Cas, bring your toothbrush."

To Caspar, Neha was a strong, charismatic woman, who liked him and who had been very loving with him. She was like something out of the forest. Was it all a matter of sex with her? Whether it was possible to be in love at his age was another thing. He had never had to consider a recreational sex or a Beauvoir-Sartre set up. Quite what was on offer he wasn't sure, nor did he know his own mind in regards to Neha. Also, he was increasingly decided on retiring from the university once his students defended. He wanted, he realized, more time for being in nature, his writing, photography, and he wanted to start painting again. He knew he would not be going back to campus wanting an office or a course to teach. Whereas Neha, he guessed, would carry on for a few more years yet as professor, which was fine by him. Caspar felt as much as he had loved his job, he needed to use the remaining years for his own activities. Being out in the woods had made him yearn for more. He'd realized it was time to cut himself loose. But thinking again of Neha, as he seemed often to do, he pictured himself in her embrace.

But towards the end of that week he had to admit he was in bad shape, shivering slightly with his prostate, sweating, in pain, burning urination, and he got an immediate appointment with his GP Dr. Helene Duchamps. "So Caspar," she said, pronounced as 'Caspere,' one eyebrow raised, "let me guess, a little too much scotch and caffeine?" She had him on the examining table, chinos and underwear round his ankles, lying on his left side, knees pulled up. Dr, Duchamp put on the gloves and lubricated the middle finger on her right hand. Casper felt her rotate her finger quickly and insert it fully into his anus. She felt around and settled quickly on the prostate, pressing a little here and there. Caspar yelped a little. "Painful no Caspar?" she said. Then she was out. Glove in bin. She told him that the gland was quite swollen and tender. "Ok, time for a reality check. You must immediately cut out all alcohol, smoking, and caffeine. Is that understood? Drink herbal tea or an occasional decaf coffee or tea. Nothing spicy. Or you will be back in hospital. You should be drinking lots of water and you should soak in warm baths, twice or three times a day. Take the ibuprofen, plus a codeine if the pain is bad, and take this prescription for an antibiotic for ten days twice a day. Book a week off and I'm serious, relax."

He liked Dr. Duchamps with her matter of fact Gallic attitude and charm. She had been his GP for twenty-five years. Putting her hand on his back she told him to come back in a week or sooner if need be.

It was Friday noon. He phoned Neha and left a message telling her he was not well and went to bed. Around seven pm his intercom buzzed. "Hello," he said quietly.

"Cas, it's me Neha, let me in." Suppressing a moan, he pressed the button.

Getting up he put on his dressing gown and opened the door to find Neha looking at him with concern. "Hi, so what's going on?"

"Oh, well you know. It's a man thing."

She came in, putting her arm around him as she entered.

"Caspar, I want to help. What's happening?"

"Well, just a moment." He left for the bathroom. Urination was agony. He had to relax his muscles to get a flow but when he did the pain made him gasp.

Coming out he said, "I can manage. It's nothing for you to be concerned about."

"Cas, tell me." Finally she got it out of him. "Ok well let's get you in the tub. Have you taken any painkillers? No?"

Neha took charge. Got him into a warm tub. Gave him the pain tablets and put the kettle on. "Ok, where's the prescription you mentioned? I'm going down to the pharmacy. Must get you started on the antibiotics."

That felt better, the warmth penetrating his lower back and nether regions, the ibuprofen and codeine kicking in. He heard the door open. "It's me," she called out. Then she knocked on the bathroom door and putting her head round, said, "How are you?"

"Better, thank you," he replied.

Once he was ensconced in his armchair dressed in pyjamas and robe, she said, "Better take this," holding out the antibiotic and water. "I'm going to make us something to eat."

He didn't object. He could hear her rummaging about in the kitchen. A strange feeling. He liked it. They sat down in the kitchen for tea. Caspar was on a cushion. "I managed to find some bread and cheese and an old tomato so its grilled cheese and tomato for us." She brought it to the table and poured each of them a cup of tea.

"Thanks Neha, it looks great." They tucked in.

"Cas, seriously, I know you aren't well. I'll come by after my class tomorrow. It's my last one. And bring in some provisions. See how you are. All right with you?"

"That would be very kind, thank you." At that point he remembered Adele would be coming in tomorrow with a few items. That's ok.

Neha took his hand and said, with concern in her voice, "I'll clear up and leave you. Take some more of the painkillers now and an antibiotic in the morning. All right?"

She kissed him on leaving and he heard the door close. He got up went again to the bathroom and climbed into bed. It was his own fault. He knew he had to be more circumspect. But he had let loose. Yet he had seen a new side of Neha. Professors, egotistical creatures that they are, were not known for their empathy. Soon he was fast asleep.

He felt pretty rough next morning, in real throbbing pain. He got up, put the kettle on and hopped to the bathroom, standing there waiting, "Jesus," he breathed, as the slow burning trickle started, stopped, started again. At times like this he wanted to get the surgery, have the thing removed and damn the consequences, but had been told by the urologist that the operation unfortunately might not get rid of the pain and he was better off at the moment staying as he was. So he stood there until the trickle stopped.

He drank tea and made toast and marmalade before heading for the shower. The warm water made him feel better. He dried off and took the painkillers and medication. His summer classes started in two weeks time in early May. Perhaps he would be well enough. He would think positive, try to do some preparation and see in a week.

Caspar read and slept and dreamed. He was back at Cambridge in an ethics seminar pretty much disagreeing with everything said. Even then he couldn't buy fully into the analytic approach. He wanted philosophy to chance its arm to actually spell out some ideas regarding what some intrinsically good aspects of life were. Then as he opened his eyes he caught a fleeting glimpse of Marjorie, this time walking in front of him at Spanish Banks Park in sandals and jeans, casting him a backward, bright-eyed glance, her lovely blonde hair flowing behind her, smiling. "Ah, Marjorie wait," he called out, but woke to his bed and the burning pain behind his scrotum.

At seven o'clock that evening the intercom buzzer went and he opened the door for Neha. "Hi love," she said as she hugged him. "How are you doing?"

"I'm fine, how are you?"

"Look I'm ok, it's you we are concerned about, how is it?"

"It's not too bad."

"Have you had the medication?"

"Not yet."

"Why don't you get in the tub. I'll bring tea and medicine."

"That would be great, thank you."

An hour later they were eating in the kitchen: roast chicken with salad. Neha was having a glass of white wine. Caspar was having apple juice. She put her hand over his and said, "Listen, I don't want you to get the wrong idea. I'm not trying to take you over, or get into your place. I'm perfectly happy where I am. I'm not your wife. But I do like you and want to see more of you when you are better, if you feel the same. Life's short you know."

Caspar nodded. He was listening but not quite. He needed to go back to bed. "You know I like seeing you. Thanks so much for being here. All these years and I never really knew you." On that he got up and said, "Sorry, I have to go," and left the table. She heard him go into the bathroom.

When he came back she said, "I was talking to my niece Rani. She knows about your condition, I hope you don't mind, and she could give you a special massage."

"Ah ha, what is it?"

"She can massage your sore area."

"What?"

"You know, your prostate."

"God Neha, I couldn't ask anyone to do that. It's sore as hell. And it would be kind of personal. I think maybe not, but thanks."

"Cas, she knows what she is doing she is a nurse. She can help. Stop being such a Canadian. I can phone her, she'll come right over. Forget about your dignity."

He felt too under the weather to object further and Rani came over that evening. She was very calm and professional. He wouldn't have believed it. She was very gentle stroking with her finger inside. Soon he was having some emissions, which she said were good, getting the juices flowing. "Also," she said matter of factly, "all emissions are good."

She was coming to see him again in a couple of days.

"So how do you feel?" asked Neha.

"Ok I think."

"Well, you know it's something she learned during her hospital training in India."

Caspar said he appreciated the care.

"Neha, how would you feel about getting in beside me for a while? No fandango just being in here together?"

"I would like that if you're sure you wouldn't just like to be alone."

"No," he said drowsily, "I'd love you to." He reached over and turned down his bedside light feeling Neha sliding in beside him. It felt nice and comforting, feeling her close up to his back. He leaned back over and touched her cheek. Soon after she put her arm across his shoulder, and they fell asleep. When he awoke next morning she was gone.

His week passed with Neha coming in every evening which became something he looked forward to. She stayed over one more night. Given her willingness to help him in this personal crisis and not be put off by his physical situation, he was feeling more comfortable with her. By the end of the week he had improved and felt he could probably teach his classes which ended in early August, though as usual he was still not totally better though the pain was not so bad. He would need around a month to fully recover. Assuming that he would. Also, he was expecting completed theses by December to be defended possibly in March or April after the editing and rewriting process. Caspar decided to arrange meetings with the students to assess their progress.

# 13

For now, he would carry on with the preparation for his courses. Some of his Asian students would be shy in class discussions, but usually by the third class or so, they would begin to join in, speak up often animatedly, give their point of view. These two undergraduate philosophy courses were very enjoyable for Caspar. He enjoyed learning about how the world was for the students, what they had to deal with, their attitudes, sensibilities and ways of relating to each other.

He was also getting no-answer phone calls with no number showing. Lots of clicks. Once, he heard someone cough. He got in touch with the phone company and they said they would look into it. A few days later, the company called back. They weren't able to identify the caller because of some weird blocking function but they did know the calls were coming from within the city. They told Caspar that they were at least able to block the calls to him, which in his mind had to be Veronica related.

A week before classes started he received a notice to come to a meeting with the Dean of his Faculty, Dr. Philippa Lindstrom. Philippa was a professor of French and Spanish language and literature. She was in her mid-forties and already a Dean. She was blonde haired, diminutive, second generation Swedish, and had a forthright demeanor. He was ushered into her office. Like Shirley, she was dressed in a two-piece business suit. Philippa, who had always struck him as pretty decent as an administrator was looking a bit straight-faced. She reached over and shook his hand. "Hello Caspar, how are you?"

"Fine Philippa thanks, how are you?"

"I'm well. Now Caspar, I have some news for you. I'm sorry to have tell you that I have decided to withdraw the graduate aesthetics specialization from the Calendar. There will not be a new intake in September. The reason is that we are going to start a new undergraduate program in Asia Studies. The Chancellor has negotiated a one million dollar grant from the Pacific Rim Foundation to help get things started. We must transfer the teaching resources in your area and from ancient history in support and as part of the general modernization of the curriculum. It was felt, given the programs in aesthetics and ancient history at VU, that people interested in these areas would still have good opportunities to pursue their interests. I'm sorry Caspar, but things are starting to change. We are, as you may know, negotiating with the government to start a new Faculty of Business and Communications. Have you had any thoughts about retirement?"

He was not often sideswiped, but now he was. They had certainly kept all this quiet. Nothing, he'd had no wind of it. Not a word from Neha either who usually knew these things. Philippa was playing it as very much a done deal. Caspar looked her in the eye and said, "But Philippa, why no consultation? This is not the way we usually do business. And what about Ronnie, has he been informed?"

"I know Caspar, but conditions regarding the securing of the grant called for strict confidentiality and we do desperately need this new program, whereas aesthetics, you know, is a small program, and like ancient history very specialized, and it was felt that these programs have very little to do with the needs of the University and the wider community these days. There is a strong feeling that we also need to move more towards the sciences and business if we are to meet the needs of British Columbians. I'm sorry Caspar. And yes, I met with Dr. Ferguson about an hour ago."

He looked at her. "Don't courses and programs for withdrawal have to go through the Faculty curriculum committee, giving people a chance to respond?"

"Yes, normally they do, of course, but it was felt, under the circumstances, I could take the Dean's prerogative on this one and make an executive decision."

Philippa wasn't looking him in the eye anymore. He wondered what Ronnie, his long time friend and colleague, would be making of all this.

Caspar looked across the desk and said, "So that's it?" Silence. "I'm very disappointed to say the least. Why the haste?" Philippa looked uncomfortable but said nothing. "Well, I will certainly have my say at Senate." At that he got up and left, knocked sideways to say the least.

He could do without this stress given how he was already feeling. He got back to his office, closed the door and pulled out the scotch before placing it back in the cupboard. So what would he do? I need time, thought Caspar. Don't say or do anything yet. Keep your own counsel. Hell! His program was about to be axed. Need to think about it. Hold on to my emotions.

Later in the week, still a bit fragile, he wrote and invited Neha to dinner to thank her for her care. The answer came back next day, "I'm sorry Caspar but I can't see you right now. I'm hosting an old friend. He 's visiting from the States. But thank you for the invitation. Maybe next week?"

Caspar was a little surprised but decided not to make anything of it. As he still had a week or so before his classes started he decided to go to Naramata and calm himself, saying he looked forward to seeing her soon and packed everything up. As he was driving he decided not to think about any of it. He would try to put his mind into free play, to echo his philosopher hero Kant. Soon he was driving through the mountains past Hope catching glimpses of the rugged peaks still snow covered.

In bed that night listening to the creek outside and the wind soughing in the trees and once an owl's hoo hoo, he curled up and fell asleep. He lay there next morning, on his back, arms above his head, breathing, in some pain, just taking in the vibes of the place. Stretched out, in his favorite room. One small window to the right of the bed, a basic paneled pine door, a bedside table and light. The room was fundamentally a box. And yet it had good feeling to it for some reason. He got out of bed and found his pipe and tobacco, which was definitely against doctor's orders. Sitting outside in the deckchair, he lit up, smelling the lovely aroma of the Dutch tobacco, always better outdoors, and took in the vista of lake, trees, sky and hillsides. After half an hour he filled the kettle and ground some coffee, decaf now, and took three ibuprofen capsules with the first cup. The antibiotics had staved off a big attack but it would take time now for things to settle down, he knew. You had to get a bit philosophical about it.

After breakfast and kitted up for a hike he set off in the Buick for the old rail line. Once on the trail, taking it steady and using his hiking poles, he looked at everything near and far. The aspen trees had their new leaves, the hillsides covered in ponderosa pine, crows cawing at him and doing some vigorous head nodding in their territory. Half an hour later, he reached the rockslide, home to a small party of ravens or was it a kindness? Already the end of April, it was bright with no wind. He stood for a while, drank some water, and breathed. Then he took out his camera, looked around carefully, and saw the great old pine tree on the lakeside edge of the path. He knew the tree but had not photographed it before. The light was good, not harsh, a little cool. He walked slowly up to the tree, a survivor of the forest fire that had swept through here ten years ago, thanks to its thick hard bark and deep roots. It really was magnificent. The bark was a deeply furrowed reddish-orange going to dark brown and black in places. The height was around twenty-five metres with branches starting about a man's height off the ground. He picked up a cone and looked carefully at its neat spiral structure. On the bark, yellow and white rivulets of hardened turpentine-smelling sap snaked down the tree. He put his hand on the trunk and stood there for a while looking up to the sky feeling gentle vibrating movements. This tree that had withstood all that nature and man had thrown at it over the past one hundred years and was, he felt, a fellow traveler.

Caspar put his arms around the trunk, which was a good two and a half metres in diameter, holding on, eyes closed. His heart rate slowed. He was ok. Stepping back, he walked all around the tree looking up and down and at what was behind it. Only then did he lift the camera. Walking back to the lakeside viewing position slightly below the tree he framed the shot in the vertical or portrait position. Bracing the camera, he breathed in, slowly let out his breath, then squeezed the button. He repeated the action changing to the horizontal landscape mode showing the tree slightly off centre in the right of the frame against a granite cliff facing up the mountain. He took a shot of the first five metres of the tree from the ground up, almost face to face with it. The tree was well lit with the afternoon sun, still fairly low on the horizon. He thought this would be a good picture sensing at the moment he had grasped something. Then he headed back down the trail for home.

That night his phone rang. It was Neha. "Cas, it's me, where are you?"

"Hi Neha, I'm at the cottage."

"Cas, I want to see you."

"Me too," said Cas. "I miss you, but Neha, I need to have some time this week to think about the Senate meeting."

"Well Cas that's one reason I wanted to see you. The word's getting around about Philippa's decision to scrap your program and Ronnie's. You know I will back you completely. We need to talk. I could fly up easily."

"Could you? You know I'm very grateful for all your care last week. That was kind of you."

"Not kind Cas for fuck's sake. It's what friends do. I'm missing you and I'm worried about you. How the hell are you?"

He loved the sound of her voice, wanting to see her. Thinking maybe he was a bit in love with her. Something had shifted in him when she had looked after him. She'd been there for him, just as Marjorie always had. God he missed her still. But now he was feeling very drawn to Neha, the more so, after their intimate times together.

"I'm much better thanks but it's rumbling on a bit. I would love to see you. How about this weekend?"

So, she came up and they had a lovely couple of days being together, walking, cooking up what food he had. They talked about the unfolding politics at the university. They squeezed into the hot bath together and snuggled up in the big bed. Caspar still wasn't well, but she did him good. Then she was gone.

Caspar sat outside in the gloaming. Not thinking. Just being there, very still, smoking. He drifted into a kind of a trance. He wasn't aware of himself. Finally getting cold and stiff, he went inside put on some heat and switched on the radio. Time for a warm soak, he thought.

# 14

That night he wrote up his field notes making reference to this sense he got when a picture might be good. It was rare, but it made the whole business worth it. He got a couple of good pictures in dozens of shots if he was lucky. His philosophical self thought it might be a case of being what it felt like when a good form suggested itself. The feeling of aesthetic pleasure Kant wrote about. Caspar remembered those individual moments, situations, where this seemed to happen for him. He knew each photograph. But what he couldn't do was plan for it in any precise or fully preconceived way. He thought there was something mystical about it. A state of awareness, divorced from the madness of the world at a moment that allowed perception to function freely. This would never stand up analytically he knew but it was real for an artist, nevertheless. And he reminded himself that philosophy was a second order activity. Without actors in the world, artists, first order people, there would be no philosophy. What would he rather be? Titian never had to worry about being academically correct, indeed that would have been a hindrance. He set his own pattern, god love him, and his works found receptive audiences over many centuries and cultures.

Wittgenstein advised his students, whatever you do don't become philosophers. Do something useful. He was turned off by the whole academic life at Cambridge. In the Second World War he became an orderly at Newcastle Infirmary. He wrote his famous Tractatus Logico Philosophicus in the trenches of the First World War, and later submitted it as his doctoral thesis at Cambridge. He gave away his inherited wealth. Caspar respected him highly. Conversely, maybe it's the old Plato thing. In his political hierarchy the philosophers were top dogs.

Phidias, the sculptor of the goddess Athena in the Parthenon was a mere tradesman. And so on down through the ages and into the modern educational system. This was one reason why, he thought, it was always easy to cut the arts courses in a squeeze. Not only, supposedly, no use to anyone or anything important, they were, artistic images, according to Plato, at a third remove from real knowledge in being copies of worldly things that were themselves copies of ideal forms that existed in some intangible mystical space.

Not only that, in Plato's ideal world the arts would be banned in case they seduced people away from his carefully crafted social stratification plan for society. Caspar naturally thought differently. He preferred Aristotle's more down to earth view that the arts could convey knowledge of human existence, universals of human experience. How else would we account for the appeal of Shakespeare's poetic tales of love and death for different peoples across the ages?

The arts, Caspar believed, were forms of understanding, languages in their own right, ways for the mind and heart to engage knowingly with the world. But the arts were not accommodating to the profit-driven utilitarian order much demanded of late. An artist had to go about things as a whole person, imaginative, intuitive, as well as conceptual. Talk only of the cognitive, of some kind of pure rational world, endlessly producing predictable results was, he knew, a crazy pipe dream. Actually it was frightening. In real life people were richly affective, idiosyncratic and flawed from the beginning. But given how the arts were viewed in many educational quarters historically as a kind of insignificant and possibly subversive play, compared with anything technical or theoretical, his and Ronnie's courses could easily be seen as dispensable.

Next morning back up the trail. The sun was beginning to pick out the rocks and leaves in a golden glow. So what to do about his program? He would go and see Shirley first thing. But he suspected it was a done deal, no going back. But he knew a big outcry could hurt the University, his home for forty years, not to mention Shirley. Was he rationalizing not doing anything? Now was when he needed Marjorie. She would help him to see his way through. Suddenly a bald eagle flew up from the path ahead making its harsh bleating cry. What was it? It was a large snake, a bull snake he thought. It was hurt but alive with a couple of big chunks missing from its side. He carefully slid his hiking pole under its middle and hoisted it off the path into the bushes. It might survive; this was the wild.

The reality, thought Caspar was that he had already decided to go, chart out a new life. Why not let them have it. He also believed that everything had its time including the aesthetics program. Programs depend for their life on particular people in place at a particular time. Everything changes. You can't step into the same river twice etc. Also, as he had come to recognize, he was getting on. He remembered a comment he had innocently made to Chas his friend last summer to the effect of "When I get old ...?" Chas had replied, "Caspar my dear friend, you are old." Really, he hadn't given it a thought. So perhaps he needn't get too angry and upset. It wouldn't do him any good. Also he didn't want to poison his mind and life with some long running vendetta in the time he had left. He had served the University well. Believed in it, supported it and his students, fought many a fight over the years, given of his best. Made himself unpopular. Maybe his body was telling him something. Time to ease off. Perhaps he could leave this one to somebody else and slip away. He could teach his own courses one more semester. Do the defences and go. Strategic withdrawal. Actually the idea appealed to him. He got on with the hike. But he would have it out with Shirley.

That evening, writing up his notes the phone rang. "Hi Cas, it's me. I wanted to tell you. My friend has left. I told him I wasn't interested in renewing our relationship. I wanted you to know, Cas. I know, it's baggage, don't we all carry some? Are you angry?"

No not angry, he was relieved to hear her voice. He assured her he wasn't and invited her to dinner for the coming Saturday, saying he wanted to thank her for all her care adding, "And it's not the same in the shower since you were here," upon which Neha breathily told him she missed it.

While on the phone Caspar was suddenly struck with the thought that he would do something about what had happened. He knew that the decision to withdraw aesthetics and ancient history would have to be given final approval by the Senate. That would be a suitable venue for him to respond. He enjoyed the rest of the week in the valley and travelled down to Vancouver Saturday morning. The retreat had given him a chance to reflect and have more time on the mountain. He was feeling a lot less rattled, though not completely pain free, and he had the photograph.

That night he picked up Neha and drove her to a small family run Italian restaurant east of the city, one he had patronized with Marjorie but he didn't say so. They had roast chicken, carrots, spring cabbage, and roast potatoes. Neha had a carafe of Soave. Caspar had apple juice. They both agreed it was wonderful, all served in a soft light and warm atmosphere. Then for desert, Neha had tiramisu and coffee. Caspar had crème caramel and chamomile tea.

Driving home Caspar said, "Look Neha, I don't want you to feel any pressure over our friendship. You have your life. I'm enjoying spending time with you, getting to know you better after all these years. Let's just see what happens. What do you think?" He was attracted to her, his feelings were coalescing, but he wasn't about to make any claims on her or acquiesce to pressure from her should she be so disposed. Quite a dance really, this idea of love in the later years.

Neha squeezed his arm and said, "That's great, but I might like to push things along a bit if you don't mind, starting with tonight if you are not busy. Can you come in? I bought you a new toothbrush"

Sunday morning at home he downloaded the image of the pine tree into Photoshop and played with processing the raw file. He tended to err on the side of less is better. Then he printed off a couple of smaller copies making adjustments each time until he put in the good archival paper and printed a larger copy on his photo printer. The picture sang. Hallelujah. The tree had an almost living presence. The picture had, thought Caspar, an elusive sprezzatura, a definite vibe not unlike the spontaneous single-stroke Chinese brush and ink calligraphy. He gazed at it and at that moment was back there on the slope taking it in, in its majesty. This print would be framed. Next day he worked on his class preparation, knowing come Tuesday, he would disappear for the next three months into summer teaching.

On Monday morning he was waiting to see Shirley James. He wanted to get her take on Philippa's move. As he entered her office she stood up and they shook hands. "How are you Cas?" She looked at him not smiling. "Sit, please."

"I'm fine Shirley, how are you?"

"Well, not great. Philippa has sidestepped the norm, but legally, I'm stuck because the policy does allow for Deans to make an executive decision and bypass the curriculum committee under exceptional circumstances. Nobody has used this policy for decades. The rationale seems reasonable on its face: modernizing the curriculum and moving resources no longer needed to support a new program coming with a large grant. But as far as I can tell there is no need for your courses or Ronnie's to be canned. From my perspective we have enough resources, together with the grant to get the program up and running. Philippa says not and she is entitled to make her own proposals. Makes me feel there's another agenda. I don't know. But we've never had a Chancellor like Adsetts. He had no business taking the lead with this Foundation. They've funded projects in other universities and the idea is good. But I'm not altogether convinced. Who is funding them I wonder? They seem flush. On the surface he's doing good for the University, moving us in the right direction. But then strangely, we have the matter of your student. I'm mulling over what I should do for the best and I'm still not sure. The Senate meeting isn't until November so there is time to work something out."

"Shirley, I think the Asia program proposal is good as long as there is no attempt to influence faculty appointments, or the curriculum, but I am going to speak at Senate as is Ronnie. Philippa seems fixed on the idea."

"Well I'm glad you are. Let's get in touch by phone if needed, by cell phone I mean. Here's my number," she said putting it on a piece of paper.

"And here's mine," said Caspar.

He started his classes, got things going, read chapters from Veronica and Cy, stayed away from the scotch and coffee, attended University committee meetings, Faculty meetings, and philosophy department meetings. He met separately with the second members for Veronica and Cy and worked at night transcribing his field notes into something more coherent. In between he read his favorite authors including now, essays by a writer on the natural history and topography of the Yukon.

# 15

In among his many thoughts about Neha, the idea occurred to him, or maybe it was not so much an idea as a stirring feeling if he was honest, that he would like to photograph her naked. He couldn't quite get the idea out of his head. During the week she kept flickering across his mind's eye. She had definitely got his juices flowing.

He wondered how, or if at all, he could broach the idea with her, and how he might start the actual photography. In his student days he had taken courses in drawing and painting from the nude, which is what you did in art school then, so he was not unfamiliar with the practice. He had the Titian book in his hand and he flicked through to the colour plate of the Venus of Urbino based on an earlier work by Giorgione, the Sleeping Venus. In both the subject is Venus, goddess of love and beauty. Both paintings feature naked females lying stretched out, one on a bed, the other on cushions facing the viewer on a gentle sloping diagonal running from left to right. Caspar then immediately thought of the Rokeby Venus by Velasquez. In this painting the subject is reclining naked but facing away from the viewer and looking in a mirror held by Cupid. Goya's Naked Maja was for him the most provocative. The subject, a woman of attitude you might say, is lying on her back, her hands tucked behind her head on the right of the frame. Her hips and torso are tilted slightly left, legs together with a small glimpse of pubic hair. She is looking out confidently at the viewer on a sloping angle from right to left. Caspar knew he was not being particularly original in considering these works but drawing on such classics was a place to start. And he knew that portraits required a collaboration. Artists owed plenty to l'art de vivre and intelligence of their models.

Neha without doubt had a physical presence. Despite being an academic, she did not live just in her head as the last few months had shown. She had invited him into a sexual liaison that had restarted his erotic imagination. He had thought all that was finished. His mind, however, was filled with impressions of her shapely body randomly arriving and fading. He decided to ignore all the controversies surrounding the male gaze and female models. For Neha and he, any photograph would be based on a free cooperation of the willing in their private and somewhat mature lives. He decided to let the idea sit for a while and see what, at the right moment, would transpire. As he was thinking about Neha, he had forgotten about the troubling matter at work. And he was feeling creatively inspired.

# 16

In the next couple of weeks Caspar met with Ronnie, a native Nova Scotian, now the only professor of ancient history, who was also feeling disenfranchised and upset at the prospect of having his program pulled without any consultation. They had started out at VU at roughly at the same time. Caspar came in straight from his doctorate at Cambridge. Ronnie came out of the Universities of Edinburgh and Toronto getting on for forty years ago. They agreed that they would each deliver a response at the November Senate meeting. They also agreed to meet with their respective Senate representatives to seek support for their position, which was the cancellation of the decision to drop their programs. Caspar was retiring soon, he knew. He felt it was the right thing for him, but now he was going to speak for the aesthetics program, which to his mind was needed now more than ever. He knew though that being irate would work against his case. In the University, calm debate was required. He would try to exhaust his anger before the meeting. A steely well-prepared mind was needed, and the garnering of as much University-wide support as possible.

That Thursday Caspar wrote to Neha inviting her to supper at his apartment on the Friday. She replied within the hour to say she would be delighted. That cheered him. He shopped for some fresh local cod and picked up a strawberry and rhubarb pie from his bakery in Kitsilano.

Caspar was in jeans, white tee shirt and sandals. Neha arrived wearing a loose pale green cotton dress, with a square neck, no sleeves, dropping to just above the knee, with a loose necklace string of blue-green sea glass shards. She had a pearl bracelet on her left wrist. She was also wearing sandals. A touch of lipstick and eye shadow finished her off. Neha hugged him at the door.

He sat her down in the kitchen and poured her a glass of wine. Told her she looked gorgeous.

On the table was a bunch of white Icelandic roses in a small matt black slightly bubbly raku vase. The table was set on a faded blue cotton tablecloth. Soon he was lifting the fish from a steamer, and draining the broccoli. He put out the food and lemon cream sauce in a gravy boat and lit a candle. Not bad he thought to himself. They tucked in. Neha complimented him on the food. They chatted taking in each other in the intimate atmosphere. Caspar was feeling comfortable. Neha put her hand on his frequently to emphasize a point. And so the dinner progressed with talk of books, walks they would do, and the possibility of another visit to the cottage. After fruit pie, warmed in the oven and served with ice cream, Caspar put on the coffee and invited Neha into the living room. "I shouldn't, but would you like one of these?" he said, offering her the American cigarettes they both liked.

She accepted and he brought in the coffee and they sat together.

"That really was delicious," she said.

He raised his eyebrows and murmured, "Good."

They sat on together in the fading light. Not saying much. Caspar gave Neha a brandy. She was due to go to Greece in July for a conference. Caspar suddenly asked, "Neha, would you be free to come to the cottage some time in August?

"Ah, Cas, thank you. I would love to but my book is promised to the publisher this summer and I still have a lot to do. I'm supposed to be working at home. I'll will see what I can do."

The evening ended and on leaving Neha kissed him tenderly on the lips. "See you soon," she whispered.

Caspar went to bed and lay thinking. He was imprinted with all the years of marriage, as was the apartment. You become almost as one, even as you try to keep some space for your own self. Sleeping together every night, little habits and affections, ways of being and loving together, decoding the subtle telegraphy. Yet marriage wasn't easy. You had to be light on your feet. Fight your corner on occasion. Neha was something else. She was a scholar of logic, respected, and highly cultivated, a lover of saxophones, and she had an amazing body. This was his last thought as he fell asleep.

# 17

Neha was busy teaching her classes for the summer semester. She was strict and demanding. The students liked her because she taught them the rigorous ways of thinking. And in teaching, everybody likes a prof who knows her field and doesn't mess about. No lates or absentees. No group work, just lectures, writing on an overhead, and questions. Better be prepared, she could be on you in a flash, sensing any faking. From her though, because she was so good in her field, crazy intelligent, nimble on her feet with wise guys, comfortable in her own skin, and full of an ineffable female essence, logic became an art form. Her classes were always filled. She received invitations to dates from some of the young guys and sometimes girls. The students gathered around her after class not wanting to let her go, asking questions, getting a charge from her presence. She would take a question or two then leave. No invitations to contact her other than office hours by appointment. And yet in the mysterious way that some teachers have to transcend pc ideas about education, she flourished. She was an autocrat but students learned important things, and fought to get in her classes.

She thought a lot about Caspar. She liked his Canadian Northumbrian cool. Bloody wasp. He was all she had learned to despise. The old white colonial, sexuality deferred, or so it had seemed. He didn't know his effect on women. She had always kept herself in check. He was married. But now it's funny, she was having to adapt to the fact that she could be more open with him, woman to man. He seemed in not bad shape physically but she felt he was not fully together emotionally. That came through to her at the cottage so redolent with Marjorie. Yet she had loved her intimate encounters with him. He was physical enough, fit from all his walking, yet in the peculiar ways of human chemistry quite feminine in some respects: gentle, affectionate, and caring. She had dropped everything to help him when he was sick yet she recognized that this was not the time to press her affections. It was not as if she was scheming to somehow overcome his resistance and win him over. Did she even want that? Well, maybe. But no, even love has its politics, especially love, and these can become insistent with age. And yet, in the shower at Naramata she had been in a state of pure physical and erotic sensation.

Neha had never thought she would be in this situation at her age. Thinking about Caspar, constantly, she felt sure that his response to her was not simply on a rebound. Yet she knew practically that there were complications. Even if he reciprocated her love what did it mean? She was functioning very well in her own life. No need to compromise with anyone. Wasn't she just too old anyway for a schoolgirl crush? But she knew it was more than that. She'd had feelings for him going back a long time. Did she want to move in with him? Maybe have to take care of him? Sometimes yes, sometimes she didn't know. Yet she couldn't put him out of her mind. He was not the first man she had been with in the past five years but he broke through her defences like no other, without seemingly trying, and she was not easy. He was so himself. He had a charisma. Maybe it was the attractiveness of him as aesthetic philosopher and artist. To a logician, Caspar represented something wonderfully unruly and unique. Not sacrificing anything for career, fame, or money. He lived very much in his own being. His work was what he was. But then again, what did she want? Ah that was the question, and with so little time to lose. Time to stop thinking. Best to appreciate what life was offering now perhaps.

# 18

Caspar and Ronnie had met with their respective Senate representatives, one per department, but had not got very far. Getting Faculty members to stand up for anything was difficult. The system rewarded compliant and self-interested individuals, and with a few exceptions they wouldn't do anything to jeopardize their own steady rise through the ranks. Both Ronnie and Caspar had operated under different principles. The biennial salary review conducted by colleagues that allowed for, of course, some revenge payback, had never been at the forefront of their concerns. They had managed to get good salaries and promotion because they were leading figures in their respective fields. Their work and stance was recognized around the world, and by key international journals and publishers. Enemies would always find weak spots given a bit of power on committees, but reputation and scholarly output was a protective shield. Nevertheless, these senators were not going to risk their necks for aesthetics and ancient history, or anybody for that matter. They would most likely go along with Philippa. Caspar phoned Shirley James to let her know they were on their own at this point. Shirley had said that they should hold steady and do nothing for now.

Caspar and Ronnie met for a pint in the student pub. They knew what to expect. Power was being exercised behind the scenes without doubt. But they were a long way from being daunted. At their stage of the game they had plenty of experience to draw upon and they basically couldn't be intimidated. Fame and riches were not their thing and they had that precious armour -- sincerity and tenure. But then as they already knew, even tenure was not absolute. At least they were not alone in this battle, possibly their last. They shook hands and promised to keep communications open by cell. Caspar watched Ronnie head back to his department. A fine man admired and respected over the years as a professor and humane individual.

Caspar spent the afternoon teaching. He got home at six and was having a cup of chamomile tea as the phone rang. It was Neha. "Hi Caspar it's me. I need to see you."

They agreed to meet at the Jericho café.

The meal was ordered with wine and apple juice. Neha clinked glasses and took a sip. "Cas I want to help you and Ronnie with this stunt Philippa is pulling. I fully support you and will attend the Senate and speak. We can't allow this. What is she doing?"

"Thanks Neha. We're getting screwed. There is apparently no urgency in cancelling our programs. The grant they will get should be sufficient to fund the new Asia program, I assume you've heard about, for a few years. I'm thinking Adsetts is involved somehow but have no evidence. There is the issue of my student. Who is behind the email she received? Veronica said she expected some pushback to her work probably from official channels. So she is not surprised."

"But what's going on with Philippa. It seems out of character," said Neha. Is she being pressured? You remember she is up for renewal in December."

"Well that makes both Philippa and Shirley then," observed Caspar "so they could both be vulnerable. But for what gain? Are we, me in particular, being got at as some kind of payback for Veronica? Ridiculous."

"You know Cas, maybe we are seeing things too much through our perspective of free speech and all that. Things are very different in China."

"So they are. Imagine if the grant were to be withdrawn for some reason; that would put Philippa in a bit of a spot. Not much we can do at the moment. The next move will be in the Senate meeting. "

"By the way," said Neha, "how are you doing health wise?"

"Better thanks. You were a great help. I know I was out of it." Looking up and putting his arm around her, taking her hand, Caspar whispered, "Come home with me tonight?"

She looked back at him, savoring the moment, the marvelous feeling of his hand on hers, his gaze on her, and nodded. "Yes, let's have coffee at home."

Later, after a long relaxing coffee, Neha excused herself and went to the bathroom. Caspar went into the other bathroom. Neha was already on the bed lying on her back, her hair splayed out over the pillow, her legs chastely together, holding out her arms out to him when he came in the bedroom. He went around to her, knelt down and kissed her. She responded with her own kiss. She was ready for him, excited, breathing. Caspar needed no encouragement.

Minutes later both catching their breath, she was looking at him. "Cas," she whispered, "I'm getting awfully fond of you."

Caspar took a breath, looked at her and said, "I know. I'm the same. You are so amazing."

The last few minutes had been life affirming and transforming. All restraint cast away. Caspar felt his very cells, muscles, and nerves resonating in harmony with hers. She looked at him, her eyes shining. They spent the night together in thrall with each other. When morning came Caspar pulled away to get up. Neha sighed and put out her arm gesturing with her hand for him to come back. He lay down again for a minute or two and she said "Cas, that was a wonderful night."

"And for me," Caspar replied getting up. "Will you come over and stay Friday night? We can have Saturday together. Go for a walk in the woods."

Neha rolled onto her back, the sheets awry, hands behind her head. She still had that fulsome glow of the night. She answered yawning, "Yes, but now I'd better get a move on."

"No, stay just as you are for a minute," said Caspar, looking her in the eye before he went out to get his camera.

Neha came to Caspar's, Friday evening. After a kiss he handed her a flat package wrapped in brown paper. She tore off the paper to find a framed black and white photograph of herself looking for all the world like Goya's nude, stretched out, unabashed. The picture was vibrant.

Neha shrieked, "Caspar! I love it, it's, brilliant, thank you. No one ever gave me anything like it," she said, as she looked transfixed at herself in the picture. He had captured her look after love, aglow, her eyes shining, hair in disarray, head and torso slightly raised on pillows, shapely hips tilted slightly left, arms behind her head, legs lying easily together down the bed, gazing back at the camera. She looked marvelous, her skin tone contrasting beautifully with the ruffled white sheets. He had signed and named it, unsurprisingly, "Neha."

"Caspar, seriously, we have to do more of these. You have caught something in me, I never saw before, you're showing me to myself. How did you do it? I'm putting it in my bedroom." That night Neha seemed unusually animated.

They had breakfast Saturday morning, then went on a long hike in the woods. Everything now was in full summer bloom. Lots of bird activity. The air perfumed from all the wild flowers, a breeze coming up through the trees from the ocean, fluttering the leaves. The weather was cool and good for walking, light filtering down through the canopy. The rest of their time together went very well. Plans were made for the following weekend.

# 19

Veronica was working in her study bedroom in her off campus digs. For the past several months now, as a doctoral candidate having passed her comps, she was at her desk every day for most of the day. Books were stacked up all around her, some in Chinese. She was trying to portray, philosophically, the value of the architecture being destroyed and the cultural crime of its dismemberment: its history, religious and cultural significance, aesthetic qualities, the experience of inhabiting these old buildings, and what such architecture meant for the local community. Veronica had grown up in a historic neighborhood, full of traditional style houses and temples. She had a first-hand knowledge about what was going on and she had brought plenty of material with her documenting the changes. She was also trying to see what relationships there were between Western and Chinese aesthetics to enable her to speak to a broader audience. What of the place of beauty? In a sense she was telling the story of the old buildings and addressing critically the impact on a society ruled by the communist party in a market economy. None of it made sense. But what then was the thesis? She felt she had to answer the question of the worthwhileness of ancient architectural culture in a contemporary society torn now as it is by greed and materialism. She could find echoes of historical contempt in the power philosophy of John Dewey, where man is the centre of all things in a context of untrammelled mastery and growth. Bertrand Russell, she read, had accused him of cosmic impiety.

So Veronica was wrestling with these issues. She was illustrating the work with some photographs of her own making. She had made cell phone videos of the outsides and interiors of buildings some lying derelict and awaiting the wrecking ball, some in the process of being demolished. She was exploring philosophical passages to be found in the ancient texts of China as sources of support. She was also reading the work of environmental philosophers, and looking at Chinese and western art for relevance, and much else, including many works on beauty.

At this point she was gathering her material, making notes sketching out the big picture, seeing how certain ideas were coalescing as possible chapters, as professor Ballantyne had taught her. Her main instrument, aside from her laptop and Word, was her fountain pen with black ink and a sketchbook of plain drawing paper. She liked the method. This way she was not glued to the computer. She could scribble little notes in a broadly visual way in the book she carried around in her purse to be transferred later. She never took her main notebook out of her study.

The physical act of writing made the work seem more personally hers. At the Art Institute, students were there to listen. Here the prof was critical, made her speak for herself, defend her arguments and claims when they talked about her work. Her concepts had to be clearly mapped out. She had to find relevant supporting literature. This approach excited her and frightened her. It was creative and asked a lot of her as author. She was committed to the line of inquiry, but sometimes doubted her ability to bring it off. Yet she felt freer in her thinking than at any time in her education.

She was, in her private moments, still worried about her own act of defiance. She knew she could reap retribution. People did, people disappeared. Nevertheless, she loved China, but did not know what the future held. For her now there was only the completion of her work. She could not think past that point. The thesis was her last thought at night and the first on waking. Professor Ballantyne had said it was the only way to get it finished. Complete dedication. But he also told his students about the importance of days off, no thinking, walking in nature. Relaxation. Letting the mind rest. Seeing a friend. Going to a movie. Even Wittgenstein took time off to watch Hollywood B movies. Caspar said that in his experience students having some down time finished on schedule more often than students who worked all the time. Because, he said, nobody could work all the time and produce first-rate writing. There had to be time for ideas to bubble to the surface.

Also, writing was not simply an act of will. You do better he said when you can relax and forget the self. Then the work flows. Writing of course depends on immersion in your subject, being prepared and having a point of view. These all take time. But there comes a time, he said, when you realize you are ready to speak. Then you write your first draft to be followed by careful editing. Remember all the students who have gone before you successfully. You are no different. Veronica reassured herself with his words.

Actually it wasn't true that Veronica only thought of her work. She also thought of Cy Russell. He made her catch her breath when she talked with him. He also listened and treated her as an esteemed equal. She thought he was very handsome in a rugged way. A real cowboy she thought. She had noticed his carved western belt and silver buckle showing a howling wolf, and boots, and had seen him wearing a cowboy hat on campus, unbelievably. She had never known a guy like him.

In the evening, Veronica liked to lie in the bathtub. This relaxed her, as she was quite an anxious person. All she had done in her life was work and study. Be disciplined enough to satisfy her mother who pushed her relentlessly at school and university. Now on her own she could let her mind wander at the end of a day's work. At such times she would often think of Cy. The way he looked at her, his strong physique and handsome face. She liked his way of being, his gentleness with strength, and wondered what it would be like to kiss him. Sometimes, feeling as though she were breaking a given order of rules she would troll through a lingerie website while wearing the scarlet bra and panties she had bought on-line, breathing in her favorite perfume, Obsession.

She was twenty-five and had opted for study instead of a husband or boyfriend. It's not as if she was feeling bitter about her situation. In China the competition is such that you have to be prepared to sacrifice much of a personal life, and she had loved her studies in art and philosophy, especially now in Vancouver. Even so she was feeling lonely. Her unsatisfied physical and emotional self was nudging her more insistently these days. Yet she would never let anything get in the way of her primary mission, never let her parents down, they who had sacrificed much on her behalf. In the bedroom, Veronica had arranged her little collection of furry creatures around her pillow, just as she had at home.

In the way of these things, Caspar decided it would be good idea to get together for lunch with his two doctoral students, so he emailed them with an invitation to meet on the following Friday at a small Chinese restaurant on Broadway. After they had met and were seated, Caspar asked if they would like chrysanthemum tea, which they did, much to the delight of Veronica. Caspar asked them to choose what they wanted from the menu. He already knew what he would be having: smoked black cod, boiled greens, with steamed rice and soy sauce. Veronica waived over the waiter and began excitedly asking him questions in Cantonese, her Guangzhou dialect. Caspar saw her face come alive in speaking her own language. She decided on pan-fried trout. Cy wanted sweet and sour chicken breast. They would eat using chopsticks. He invited them to have a glass of wine, which they accepted with thanks. He was having apple juice.

Caspar knew them both quite well by now. The purpose of the meeting was to get together outside of the work environment, socialize, and generate some good feeling. During the lunch they could share concerns and hopefully release some of the tension that can build up during the thesis writing. They got through the polite greeting stage and asked him about the defence. He gave them a brief rundown and said that closer to the event, and depending on the examination committee, he would speak to each of them with advice and recommendations for the procedure but not to be concerned at the moment. He would find suitable external examiners and discuss the choices with them. They trusted him. He had a good track record as a thesis supervisor, which included getting students through the defence.

But as he always told his students at the time, we do our best but in the event there can be no guarantees. Take it easy. I'm there for you. What he doesn't say is that examiners can sometimes leave go of their fair-minded senses and go off on some personal bent or theoretical bias, often with little relevance to the thesis. Second members can reveal hidden resentments and attack their own student. God forbid. There is no knowing. But he hadn't lost anybody yet. His job as senior, well there will be time for that later.

The lunch was very enjoyable. Veronica spoke up with interesting anecdotes from Guangzhou, and some of the more unusual culinary choices. She had grown up living on the thirty-third floor of a forty-storey apartment block. Her father had been a policeman, her mother a nurse. But in their youth they had been Red Guards. It wasn't a choice and had been pretty awful. Especially being sent out to the country to work on the farms and be educated by the peasants. She was of course an only child. Cy's childhood couldn't have been more different growing up on the ranch. Veronica listened absorbed as he told them about his love of horses, the vast ranges of grasslands, the seasons and wild life.

Caspar told them about being born on a sheep farm in Northumberland and moving to Canada. And about playing rugby, and studying art. They were all ears. They knew about Marjorie and tactfully never asked about his personal life. He liked both of them, so seemingly different. They would be a good pair to finish up his working life with. The lunch ended on a good note, Caspar thought. He might be getting old but he did think he detected a spark or two between his guests. They both watched and listened intently as the other spoke and often responded with a laugh or two. Quite animated he thought.

That night he got an email from Veronica asking if she could phone him at home. The matter turned out to be that her funding had been stopped. She could get no response from the education committee back in Guangzhou. Caspar told her he would do what he could to help her. He reached Shirley by cell later that night and was relieved to be told that she would provide a subsistence grant. It looked as if Veronica was getting some retaliation. What were they up against? "How is she holding up?" asked Shirley.

"She seems steady enough," said Caspar. "Stoic actually. She said at the beginning there might be some repercussions."

# 20

Cy felt both disturbed and excited after the lunch. He had been wanting to see Veronica again. But he had never had so much as a glimmer from her. She seemed totally preoccupied by the work. At the lunch though he had been sitting next to her, breathing in her perfume, casting glances her way, more directly when she was speaking. He was sure he'd been getting some subtle vibes from her. Could that be right? She had looked right at him and smiled, maybe for the first time. He felt it. That night he emailed her with an invitation to go for a walk the following Saturday. Take a leaf out of the prof's book. She replied an hour later in the affirmative. Cy whooped as he read the email. They would walk the seawall looking out for the otters, then go for lunch.

The week following the lunch with the prof, Cy was working on his thesis up at the ranch, coming for a visit to see his parents. He loved the clean wind and wide undulating vistas, creeks, ponds and lake, and stretches of pine woods, aspen, cactus and sagebrush. He rode out often on horseback by himself. Taking photographs, enjoying the change from academic work but always finding he needed to make a note or two. The ranch was almost a hundred and forty years old. He had grown up living in an original log cabin, able to ride when he was five. His parents Frank and Celine Russell owned and ran the ranch of twenty thousand acres, inherited from Frank's parents, with three thousand Hereford cattle. There were two long serving live-in ranch hands whom Cy had known since birth, Arthur and Cornell, a Nicola First Nations guy, Jesse, who was married with two children and lived down by Quilchena, and a fellow from Kamloops, David, each with his own string of five quarter horses.

Many of the old customs on the ranch continued. They bred their own cattle and horses, did all the shoeing, fencing, and metal fixing. It was a cowboy ranch with all the herding done on horseback with the aid of half a dozen black and white Border Collies. The shepherds in Northumberland would have been amazed at their beloved collies herding cattle. Cy's mother, with help from a young First Nations woman, Billy, a cousin of Jesse's, did the cooking and fed everybody breakfast, a packed lunch and thermoses of coffee, and then a hearty supper in the main house kitchen around six pm. In winter, Arthur and Cornell, who had lived on the ranch all their adult lives and were now in their fifties sometimes wore the wool chaps as of old.

It was a way of life now increasingly influenced by the need to diversify and take in guests. Ranch tourists. His parents had built two special cabins for that purpose. Visitors could go fly-fishing on the lake if they so wished, for cutthroat trout. Cy loved the ranch and his parents, who had supported him all through his life, and later his studies. But he was feeling very unsure of his life's prospects. He was inspired by his studies, by the professor's open and creative way of doing philosophy. Cy wanted to teach in the university. Nothing had been said but he knew his parents were hoping he would take over the ranch. He spent many hours worrying about the future. But his priority was to complete the PhD. Then he would see.

He was drawn to all the forms of nature around the ranch: everything from a great variety of small birds to the raptors including owls, hawks, eagles, and ospreys, to moose, deer, elk, wolves, black bears, cougars, bobcats, coyotes, badgers, porcupines, snakes, butterflies, western toads, and to the trees, flowers and grasses. The seasons, light, air and weather were a lifelong fascination. He loved swimming in the lake and had fished when younger. He had an impulse to write in a critical way about what could be a disappearing way of life as farming and ranching became more industrialized. How long the ranch could sustain itself on an old-fashioned family basis was uncertain.

Cy wanted to create a picture of the ranch and its customs and values before it was too late, and to identify and show its aesthetic qualities. But also he wanted to examine the negative side of the ranch for the animals and environment, and in a frank way deal with the costs to the local First Nations people of the ranch's presence and history. He was reading widely from environmental philosophy, aesthetics, First Nations writers, books from a few favoured women philosophers writing about ethics, gender, and literature, and the classical works, from novels, and searching through the old newspapers and writings from the locality.

He intended the work to be a philosophical biography of his life experiences, his fascination with natural history and love of horses, and his awareness that it had all come at a cost. He remembered competing on weekends for saddles in high school rodeo meets. Showing off their prize bull. But within a few years the world of the web, the global economy, and the need to be skillful in technology was drawing kids away. Cy was pretty much on schedule with his thesis. He had drafted out three and a half chapters and had a good idea overall of where he was going. He wanted to have further meetings with his second member Jeff Matthews to consult with him about indigenous issues.

# 21

Caspar was entering the last month, July, for the summer classes. He was doing his marking, preparing lectures and class activities. Thinking ahead to August. He had an idea for a photography project involving water and the landscape. The subject would be something to do with rivers and streams in the Okanagan valley, and of course the lake. In August everything would be baked so the temperature and weather would be part of it, producing a certain kind of light best encountered from dawn to about nine or ten o'clock in the morning and then from around five to whatever time at night. Each day would be planned for area, topography, and entering water habitats.

In the Eastern philosophies, great respect is given to water, to streams that flow down mountainsides unhindered, over and around obstacles with the power of yin, a feminine quality associated with the valley and water. This year he wanted to use a small waterproof camera and immerse himself in the flow and depths of streams and use his SLR for everything else. Caspar never used a tripod. He found it too static and limiting, and it had to be carried. He felt he could be more spontaneous with a hand held approach. Naturally the thought of time in the cottage, doing photography, being out in the wild, was getting him excited. A pile of boots, backpack, cameras and lenses, hiking poles, clothing, books and maps was growing in the spare bedroom.

He told Neha of his plan for August and said she should come even for a few days. She could still work. On that basis, space to work during the daytime, she thought she would be able to squeeze in three or four days in the second week. Caspar had a plan to take her to a special and very private beach, accessible only by boat, for an overnight camp. He had also been working in a preliminary way on a project on urban sites of nature, trees springing up in parking lots, small ponds, birds' nests, allotments, wasteland, nature reclaiming derelict buildings, bridges, small bits of woodland, etc.

# 22

Veronica and Cy had their walk on the seawall. She had on a long pale blue cotton dress with sleeves fastened at the wrist, a small vee neck, and low heel red shoes. Her black hair underneath a wide brimmed straw hat was falling free down her back and around her face. She had on a little eye make up and a trace of dark lipstick. Cy had greeted her with a brief kiss on her cheek, noticing the small dark fuzz of hair on the nape of her neck and absorbing her perfume. She looked up at him, their eyes meeting for the briefest of seconds before she put on a pair of silver rimmed sunglasses.

Nothing had prepared him for this. He felt a tremor in his body in being so close and wanted to embrace her. But no, he pulled away. He was wearing still blue but battered jeans, a washed-out red tee shirt un-tucked, beat up Birkenstocks, sunglasses and blue baseball cap. As he engaged her more in conversation, smelled her perfume, cast glances at her, he felt himself even then, being more drawn to her. She was beautiful in a way he had not known before. Her eyes especially, and she had an amazing mind. He loved the way she moved, gliding almost, and looked him in the eye. She told him more about her life in Guangzhou, her parents, and spoke animatedly about the differences she found with Vancouver. She loved the freedom and more laid back attitudes but her impression was that life in Canada was easier. They talked a bit about their work and their anxieties regarding the defence. Under the big suspension bridge spanning the water between the Park and the North Shore they saw some otters playing by the water's edge, which delighted her.

They sat and leaned for a while against a log on Third Beach and had a coffee. Cy told her that it was a good place for swimming as the beach dropped off quickly into deeper water. She replied that if this had been Guangzhou every small piece of the beach would have had a person on it. At the end of their day she said goodbye and shook his hand. He didn't want the day to end but didn't push it. He would give her a day or two before getting in touch.

# 23

The semester ran down to its close. Everyone was anxious to get out of the place. Caspar put in his grades and that was that. His students had applauded him on their last class. He had enjoyed their quick minds and good nature. Except for two fails. Now at the beginning of August he would go up to the cottage on the Saturday. He had to be back in a couple of weeks to prepare his classes and attend department meetings for the Fall.

On Saturday morning with good spirits he set off in the Buick. Now in shorts and tee shirt, he listened to a politics program as he drove along, dodging big trucks and families towing holiday trailers. Occasionally a squad of Harleys would overtake him, the riders kitted out in their club regalia. What kind of life would that be, he wondered, on the edge of society or so it seemed. He loved the idea of motorcycles, their glamour and throbbing beauty was hard to resist. But you can't have everything.

Early on the Monday he dragged his eighteen-foot aluminum boat to the water's edge and loaded up. He started the little outboard motor and headed slowly up the lake north towards Kelowna for about an hour until he reached the edge of the desolate Mountain Park on his right. He was kitted out for an overnight stay. The big lake was smooth, the mountains on either side craggy and wild, the air scented with the early morning water mist.

Feeling the dawn sun on his back he reached his destination, a small beach partially hidden by a rocky outcrop known as Bear Island. He steered the boat until it scraped onto the gravelly sand, removed his runners and climbed out to pull it onto the shore. Behind him a few yards in was a sheer granite cliff a good hundred feet high making access to the beach by land, impossible. The beach was a strip of sand about one hundred yards long by around twenty yards deep. There was nothing on it except sand, driftwood, what looked like a cluster of sage bushes, and a few other unidentified green leafy bushes. Caspar fastened the boat to a log, looked around and sat down, gazing out at the lake. Already his breathing had changed. He just absorbed his surroundings. Watching the swallows catching midges, and an osprey gliding overhead, probably nesting in the cliff. What an amazing place. He never tired of it. He lay back and looked up at the sky, nothing but blue and high cirrus clouds.

After unloading and setting up the small tent he stripped off everything and waded into the water. It was cool and welcoming. There was nothing to beat it. He felt the water caress his skin. Gradually he got into the deep water and swam for a while, breast stroke, until stopping to float on the surface on his back, letting himself just hang in the water. The sensation of the water on his body, the sun's rays, the feeling of just being there, in the moment, helped to dispel some of the neuroses of the academic life, the emotional asceticism of too much living in the head. After a while he swam slowly back, relishing using his muscles and limbs and feeling the depths beneath him, spitting out lake water, dipping his head below the surface as he kicked and glided forward. Soon he was wading back to shore. He dried off, dressed and was ready to take on the day. Thinking of Neha. He would bring her to this treasured spot. He got out his small single burner propane stove and boiled water for tea.

Sitting on his low beach chair he lit his pipe. He remembered the trip to Haida Gwaii, ancestral home of the Haida people, he had taken with Ronnie a few years ago, just the two of them on a jaunt. Staying in an old log B & B by the beach all meals included. Sitting out one night together on old style folding wood and faded canvas deck chairs in the sand dunes facing Hecate Strait, they had lost track of time, talking philosophy and history, or so he remembered. It was magical, the stars aglow in the vast firmament above the dark island, reminding them both of their insignificance, the sound and smell of the ocean. The owner's dog, an old yellow Lab lying cheerfully asleep at their feet. They had got slowly drunk on scotch and fallen asleep to wake with the golden dawn light streaming into their faces from across the water. Their hostess came out with steaming mugs of strong dark coffee. Truly memorable.

They had made their way up to Massett on the northern tip of the island, seats booked for the flight over to Prince Rupert on the mainland. That day he remembered, the weather was closing in. The airline staff had hurried them on board the plane, a sixty year old de Havilland Beaver five seat sea plane and they took off just as the storm was sweeping in from the west. From six hundred feet Caspar watched below as they flew over a long, curving, peninsular strip of sand stretching out to sea, the northernmost tip of the island. They kept barely ahead of it, the storm, marveling at the sight of a dark ocean, tumbling black clouds, shafts of brilliant light and sweeping rain. The pilot, wearing the company baseball cap with "Pacific Seaplanes" across the front, just a kid or so it seemed. Landing, the company closed off all flights.

Caspar and Ronnie spent the night in a small wooden hotel by the docks, eating fried fish so fresh it melted in their mouths served with large chips and local draught pale ale, before heading south to Prince George next day on the train. Their carriage was pure nineteen fifties Canadian Pacific shiny aluminum, beautifully fitted out, with a small bar, waiter, and an upstairs viewing compartment. Ronnie and he had oyster soup and a glass of white wine before settling into their seats upstairs to view the magnificent mountains and rivers gliding past them. Some long dead author once said the past is a foreign country. Maybe so but this can be hard to accept when trolling through memories that assume a greater significance as we age, all a part of life's journey. A kind of slender not exactly linear whole, with gaps, but with certain scenes drawing us back in irresistibly, performances, events, hallmarks of fate and character seared into the velvet fabric. It all seems like yesterday. Must be the case for everybody. Caspar was still living under the aura of Marjorie, probably always would be. If he could he would bring her back to life. Selfishly perhaps, he'd always imagined dying with her lying next to him, arms around him, whispering words that had meaning only for them. Telling him she loved him. No one else could fill this role. It takes forever to build up such a deep affective relationship and history.

Caspar had a great day on the beach. He enjoyed his own company. He took photographs of the cliff, the water lapping on the shore, the light on the landscape, everything. Later he got into the water with his waterproof camera and spent an hour swimming, wading up to his neck, diving down, taking pictures from all angles, inward to the beach, partially submerged, collecting rays of light going through the water. He even took some shots of himself, naked in the water. So the day passed. He wrote in his field notes many observations the way the wind seemed to pick up over the water north to south every day around four o'clock making waves, the heat, the sky and clouds, everything.

That night in his sleeping bag around three am he heard something, barely, a scratching, he listened, holding his breath, then again, outside the tent. He slowly and cautiously unzipped the bottom section of the entrance and looked through the narrow opening. There in the moonlight about twenty yards away, a cougar was standing staring back at him. Caspar remained absolutely still looking at the big mountain lion covered in tan and brown fur. How did it get there? He had never seen an animal, apart from snakes, on that beach. Maybe it had smelled something downwind and swum around the big rock? He had once spotted a cougar swimming in the lake. Caspar reached back into the tent for his backpack and found the camera. He set the speed on high and opened the lens wide. Slowly and quietly he raised the camera and framed the animal. The shutter was set on quiet mode. He sat still, marveling at the sight and gently pressed the shutter. Just to be safe he found the bear spray and unlocked the trigger. Finally dawn arrived and the sun slowly illuminated his stretch of beach. When he looked again the animal was gone. To where and how he didn't know.

Caspar climbed back into his sleeping bag and slept for a couple of hours. He was starting to get that feeling of being alive in his body that the wild outdoors can bring. He lay awake for a while then got up to make tea and eat some fruit. He packed up and headed for home in the late afternoon. That night he wrote about the visit of the cougar.

As he travelled about tracing the streams shown on the map, and hiking to explore suitable spots for photographs, he smelled the hot dry tree resin particles of the forest, and let the leaf-dappled sunlight wash over him. How to put that in a picture? Using his wide-angle lens he spent his days becoming more at one with the land, and with his waterproof camera at one with the water. He immersed himself in cold mountain streams taking photographs as the water swirled around and over him.

He felt himself at times becoming detached from the iron grip of his conceptual framework, in a zen-like trance where the world shone with a crystalline brilliance. It took him in. He found it hard to return to the world of human construction. He had a feeling of intense happiness as he repeated his actions unthinking. He wrote later that he felt the earth had welcomed him to a place of pure being.

Later he travelled south a few miles to join the Okanagan River running full and clear even in the summer. Going down the river path the first morning he noticed something, dark hanging by a thread from a tree branch by the river. On closer inspection he realized it was a bat hooked on a fishing line. Moving quickly, he pulled the branch down and cut the filament, leaving the small hooked bat in his hand. Next he pulled gently on the hook, then giving it a twist got it free from the bat's mouth, drawing some blood. The bat looked at him its eyes and teeth glistening. Caspar looked back at the little creature encased in his hand, so wild, then launched it into the air, glad not to have been bitten. It took flight immediately. Caspar could only assume the bat had been attracted to some bait on the hook of a snagged line and in taking it became hooked itself.

Soon after, Caspar was swimming in the river moving by breast stroke through the pools and eddies gliding underwater over river trout hovering in the current, at the edge of the river's main flow, waiting for morsels to swirl past, using the little camera to capture the scenes of life. Then astonishingly, a large green toad about the size of a baseball, swam by him, then under him, showing clearly its legs and webbed feet stretching out, pulling, and kicking through the depths, moving slowly enough to allow Caspar a couple of close up shots. This beguiled him beyond words.

Caspar knew that there was a body of opinion that said his kind of photographic work was useless and ethically remiss, in not revealing the true extent of the earth's degradation, pollution, global warming, the rape of the earth for greed, or indeed the extent to which animals were being brought to extinction cruelly to satisfy ridiculous human needs. Sympathetic as he was to this point of view, he felt that as there were plenty of photographers doing that already he could take another perspective, one that shows what we are at risk of losing, the beauty of nature and landscape as an inspiration towards a more appreciative and loving stance. His rule was not to photograph anything that could appear on a postcard, or photograph in a way that had a commercial look. Not that he was altogether against it. Rather he aimed ideally for amateur work produced by his own sight and feelings, sought by getting into places on his own feet. Becoming immersed for a length of time in a place. Getting to know it in some depth, in different weathers and times of year, revealing qualities as he had experienced them. While he worked relatively close to home, he respected and admired the dedication of photographers who went into the world's far corners, such as Sebastiao Salgado, to show vestiges of the unspoiled planet. Caspar simply wanted the work to be his own.

He got a call from the phone company that evening to tell him the no-answer phone calls couldn't easily be tracked because they were backed by some pretty sophisticated software and that they had never encountered anything like them before. But the technician, making an informed guess, thought they originated in Vancouver, which set Caspar thinking. But now at least the calls would be blocked.

Caspar's Rivers and Streams pictures were to be exhibited in the University Library in December. He was busy every day creating his portfolio. Up early, getting the light, walking into different areas of the mountains. He was feeling fitter by the day. And every day involved immersion, wherever he was, or in the lake when he got home. Neha would arrive on Sunday for four days. He was looking forward to it. They would camp overnight at the little beach. Good things to come. He would invite her now to the September concert of the Baroque Ensemble, a performance of Purcell's Dido and Aeneas.

# 24

While he was writing his notes in the evening he drifted into the area of his undergraduate class in the fall, "Philosophy and Art." Some of the key questions were, as he wrote, what does it mean to understand a work of art, particularly one from the past? And, what does it mean to appreciate a work of art? This led him to three generally held ideas: one that a work of art passes the test of time if it has some great distinctive quality, and if it can sustain interpretations that embody the viewpoints of successive periods. Or, two, a work of art passes the test of time on the basis of an interpretation that would have been made by its original audience — that is, one in accord with the artist's intentions. An artwork, like a passage of speech, is something produced by design. It cannot logically mean whatever successive audiences deem it to mean, so the argument goes. Or, three, a work of art is something visual. Its meaning does not come down to scholarly interpretations but to a visual language, to seeing what is before you in paint. What then does it mean in such a case to speak of understanding and appreciation? This year he would make extensive use of art from the renaissance–baroque periods including the work of Titian, Artemisia Gentileschi, Rembrandt, Rubens, Claude Lorraine, Velasquez, and with Turner thrown in because he liked him, also to introduce his students to this marvelous tradition of art, which would in any case prompt all manner of critical questions, disagreements, objections, and possible delight. The students would have to make up their own minds and present answers to questions arising. Here was where Caspar was pleased by what was on offer from the web. He could call up virtually any artwork on the data projector in a second. Long gone are the days when he was restricted to a single, small, and very expensive set of slides. In galleries nowadays he took lots of photographs for use in his classes. Also, in cases where assignments involved photography or drawing, students could project their work with ease for the whole class to see and discuss.

# 25

The next day, Sunday, Caspar went to the airport to pick up Neha. She was looking summery in a light grey and blue floral dress and sandals. He could smell her perfume, the same sandalwood aroma. Unusual as a perfume thought Caspar but entirely right in this case. They chatted in the car, effervescent. Sharing that they were glad to see each other. Neha had her hand on his neck as he drove, pushing her fingers into his hair. It was baking hot, dry and dusty. All around, the vineyards and orchards were verdant, watered and richly green, the fruit visibly swelling. At the cottage Caspar suggested a swim. In a moment Neha saw him heading for the lake au naturel and as quickly as possible she herself disrobed and rushed into the water. The lake was welcoming and cool. "Cas, this feels fantastic," she said, as she swam away from shore.

Caspar came up from behind and pulled her to him. Caressing her body, made more alive in the water. "God, does anything feel better than this?" he said, as he kicked out in the water to stay afloat.

At that moment she struck out for shallower water, then as he swam up in her wake and stood on the sandy bottom, she turned to face him, putting her arms around his neck and wrapping her legs around him, buoyant. How good it felt skin on skin, being so close. Somewhat reluctantly they waded ashore and into the warm shower. Caspar decided the sun was over the yardarm and made a gin and tonic with ice and slices of lemon for Neha and half a glass of white wine for himself. Condensation was running down the glasses. He took one into the bedroom for her.

"That looks so good, thank you. And that was a wonderful welcome if I may say. Has to be repeated at least once a day.

Seriously," she said, getting up close, arms around him and pausing to kiss him luxuriantly on the lips, "it's so great to see you, you feel so good, and look how brown you are," she said, putting her arm against his.

He was feeling again the physical buzz of well-being he knew of old. He smiled at her and squeezed her bottom, which elicited a little squeal and suggested a sit on the veranda. Neha put on a wrap, Caspar in his shorts and tee shirt. At this time of day, mid-afternoon, the sun was over the end of the cottage, which fortuitously was sheltered by the sizable cottonwoods bordering the creek giving ample shade. They had an hour chatting, looking at the colourful birdlife flitting from tree to tree, watching as an osprey returned to the massive nest high in a tree opposite, beak loaded with fish for her now sizable chicks.

The few days together were marvelous for the pair of them. They had so much to talk about regarding the local environment, books, their swims, art, music, cooking, wine, news, radio programs, politics, and so on. It was a liberation being together. Really, a gift, never expected, but recognized by both for what it was. Feeling free now, to be more fully themselves. Neha got on with her work. Caspar went out into the hills. Time did not permit the overnight camp but it was registered for the future. She would go with him to the concert in December. How amazing it was to have a baroque orchestra right in their midst playing on instruments requiring gut strings.

Caspar had long realized he believed in the historicist version of artistic understanding and appreciation. And though few would agree with him he wanted the magic of an experience in accord with the period of inception, as intended for its original audience. For him that was the point. To get on the inside of a form of life and sensibility related to ours in being human but also one having a different taste. There was he knew, no prescribed method to achieve this other than by responding through one's instincts and imagination, and no direct method of checking for authenticity. But still, art was like that. And that was part of its magnetic allure. It touches us with a truth we recognize but cannot fully explain and it does so with emotional resonance.

The time at the cottage came quickly to an end. Neha had left a week ago after a pivotal time for the pair of them. They had developed a very loving link. They had played. As well, Caspar felt he had made plenty of images to work with. He was looking forward to the fall semester, the Senate meeting notwithstanding. He would give it all he had. Thoughts were going through his mind for his response. God knows whether they could pull it off, defeat the motion. Caspar knew that the aesthetics program was an emblem of who he was, of all he felt and believed. He had put his life into it.

On that note he was surprised to receive a letter from the environmental aesthetics journal telling him that not only was his article accepted but that they wanted to enter the work for consideration for a prize given by London University for the best international article in philosophy of art for the year. He was pleased they had accepted the article but not sure about the award. He didn't think that scholarship was a competition. Maybe Neha would be able to advise him. Of course, as he thought about it perhaps it might not be a bad thing to have such prestigious recognition for his work at this time of challenge for the program. Neha gave him precisely this response. She thought it would be wise to accept the nomination. So he thanked the editors and told them they could go ahead with the award application.

Now in the fourth week of August and Caspar was fully into course preparation. As well he was looking at his new pictures. In the late afternoons he darkened his study at home and switched on his computer. He had already downloaded the water pictures and had a good look through them. He thought he would need around thirty 16 x 10 inch pictures in colour. The Library would select one image from the group as the poster work to be printed in a lab.

This was a rewarding stage for an artist. Identifying the images he would work on. Some pictures revealed themselves slowly. Others lost their buzz with familiarity. Caspar did his photo editing with a light touch, then made a first print. Would it work? As the paper slid forward on the tray Caspar lifted it out careful not to touch the surface, which needed some time to dry. He placed it on a side table and looked at it. It showed the water of a mountain creek tumbling along from just half under the surface with the forest around, and sky, looking downwards into the flow. Caspar sensed an alive, vibrant energy in the golden early morning light. A keeper.

He worked at the pictures each day following his course preparation. He usually managed to process and print one picture, sometimes two. On other occasions he got nothing. It occurred to him as he was working to email Cy and Veronica to make sure they were backing up their work on a memory stick. Caspar could remember, in the days before computers, he had only one thesis script typed out bit by bit on an old Royal typewriter plus a carbon copy. There were stories of students leaving completed theses on buses that were never to be seen again.

# 26

Cy had met up with Veronica twice more for walks and coffee, but that was it. He was just as busy as she. Nevertheless, he wanted to see more of her. He had the idea to invite her to a weekend at the ranch. She replied to say that she would like to go but would need to think about it. She too was affected by her feelings. Even more so since she had seen him again. She wrote back to accept but said it could only be for two nights. They set out from Vancouver at one o'clock Friday afternoon in Cy's SUV driving east through Hope and onto the long stretch of the Coquihalla highway through the mountains. Veronica sat taking it all in, with frequent intakes of breath. As a big city girl she had never seen such vast ranges of snow-covered mountains, with virtually no human settlements in sight. Cy stopped the car periodically for Veronica to have a better look.

After a couple of hours on the road he took the plunge and asked her if she had a Chinese name. Veronica was quiet for a moment then said 'Meifeng,' which means beautiful wind. When I was at school and learning English, we were allowed to choose an English name and I chose Veronica. That is what I would like to be called."

Eventually they dropped down into Merritt, a small western town with a classic old hotel and drove up the old road going north east to Kamloops. Cy told her that this was an area of several large cattle ranches. Theirs was one of the smaller ones, founded in 1885. After forty-five minutes travelling past high bluffs and Nicola Lake, named after a First Nations chief, they branched off right and soon came to a large wooden gate with an overhead sign saying "Russell Ranch." After another fifteen minutes they pulled into an area of farm buildings, log cabins, barns, and corrals. A couple of dogs, border collies that worked with the ranch hands herding cattle, ran up barking.

So the weekend began. Veronica met Cy's parents, Frank and Celine, who welcomed her warmly. Celine showed her up to her room asking her if she had ever been in this area before and asking about her parents. Then she and Cy went off in the jeep to explore. That evening they enjoyed Celine's cooking in the big kitchen. The next morning, Cy asked whether she would like to go for a horseback ride. Amazingly she did, wearing a pair of borrowed boots that she liked for making her taller. Being small it was quite hard for her to get astride the animal. Helped up into the saddle her senses taking in the height, feeling the power of the animal and the smell of horse and old leather, she learned how to manage the reins western style, and was allowed to ride slowly around the corral. Later she and Cy went by jeep to see some of the cattle on the range being tended by two of the cowboys, Arthur and Jesse, and three of the collie dogs. She found it all quite magical never having seen such things before. She couldn't believe all the space for so few people. That night they had a barbecue back at the ranch. It all went by quickly. Cy's mom and dad wondered what it all meant.

Returning to Vancouver, Cy pulled up outside her apartment on the Sunday evening before handing her a wrapped package. "What? What is this?" she said in her unique voice.

"Open it, they're for you," said Cy.

Veronica was a little nonplussed. But inside the box was a pair of light brown suede women's cowboy boots, with tassels at the sides from near the tops. She looked across at Cy and down at the boots. "I am so surprised Cy. Thank you very much. They are beautiful." She felt the suede, "You are so kind." With that she leaned over, put her hand on his, and kissed him gently on his lips, "And thank you for the lovely weekend."

Cy put his arm around her shoulders and returned her kiss. "You know, it was great for me too."

At that Veronica pulled away and got out of the car. Cy helped her to the door with her bag. "Let me know if the boots don't fit. It would be easy to change them."

A few days later, Veronica received an email from Cy telling her about the proposed withdrawal of the ancient history and aesthetics programs he had heard about from a friend. Word was getting around.

# 27

Just as Caspar was getting up one morning the phone rang. As he answered he heard a couple of funny clicks. First silence, then a man's voice faintly, "Hello, Caspar, it's your cousin."

"What? Who? Oh, Robert? How are you?"

"Well, I've been better. I'm in the Infirmary at Newcastle. I'm almost finished. Cancer. I wanted to tell you that I'm leaving you the farm."

"The farm?"

Caspar was trying to take it in and understand the accent, a bit like the Scottish and familiar.

"I don't have long Cas."

"God Robert, why didn't you tell me sooner?"

"Ah it's fine. I've no regrets."

"I'll come over and see you. I'll get the plane tomorrow."

"No Cas, you won't have time. It's been a great life with the animals. I hope you find everything to your liking. I'll say goodbye. Take care of Cynthia." Then he hung up.

"Robert. Robert, wait." But the line was dead. Caspar got the number of the hospital and phoned.

They put him through and someone said, "Palliative Care."

"Hello, yes, I'm phoning about Mr. Ballantyne, my name is Caspar Ballantyne, I'm in Vancouver. He just talked to me."

"Yes, I know, I'm his nurse, Mary." All in a melodious Caribbean lilt.

"Can you tell me please, what's his situation? Do I have time to fly over?"

"I don't think so. He is in the final stages now not feeling any pain. He comes and goes. The doctor thinks it's only hours. He's a lovely man."

"Thank you for speaking with me. I'll phone again, see if he can talk to me. May I leave you my number? Thank you, thanks."

Caspar sat there in his living room, a bit stunned. The last time he had seen Robert was when he was a student at Cambridge. At his parents' urging he had paid his grandparents and uncle's family a visit at the farm. Prior to that he had only seen Robert once, aside from when they were young children, when he was about fifteen, visiting Northumberland with his parents.

He stayed home during the day. Later, around ten pm the phone rang and in that distinctive Geordie accent, a woman's voice said, "Hello Mr. Ballantyne, this is Christine from the Newcastle Infirmary, Robert's nurse. I'm phoning to tell you that your cousin Robert passed away at three am this morning. It was very peaceful. His friend Cynthia was with him."

"Oh, I'm sorry to hear that," said Caspar.

"Oh no Mr. Ballantyne. Robert was ready to go. He said he'd been very fortunate and had no regrets. How many of us can say that? He has a few possessions here, some books, clothes, his watch, and some photographs. Would you like us to send them?"

"Yes, I would, thank you. I will send you the postage."

"No no it's fine. We can do it. We'll all miss him. He was a very special person. Goodbye then."

"Just a moment, what about the funeral arrangements? I would like to help."

"No it's all right, Robert's friend Cynthia has it taken care of, the cremation. Goodbye then." The phone clicked off.

Caspar couldn't quite take it all in. He never cried but he did now, whether for Robert or himself or both he didn't know. But something deep within him had moved. He felt numb. Then he remembered Cynthia. He'd seen her on that visit from Cambridge. She must have been about his age. Came up to Ballantyne's driving a tractor with a couple of collies in tow. Quirky looking, hair back, a bit scruffy in jodhpurs, tallish, slight of stature, tanned, with prominent blue eyes and a longish nose and thin lips. Didn't really notice him.

A few days later he opened a letter from Willoughby & Wright, Solicitors, Jesmond Chambers, Blackett Street, Newcastle upon Tyne, UK, informing him that his recently deceased elder cousin, Robert Alfred Ballantyne, had left him Jupiter farm, the Ballantyne family farm, in the Tarset Valley, in the county of Northumberland. He was Robert's last surviving relative. This included fifteen hundred acres of freehold land, an eighteenth century four-bedroomed stone farmhouse, one shepherd's cottage, several stables, small outbuildings, and vehicles, plus various ancient trees, orchards, and furniture, books and artefacts, therein, in their entirety. The balance of the estate, fifty-five thousand pounds in cash is left to Mrs. Cynthia Oughtershaw of Ravensburn Farm. He sat down not really taking it in. The letter went on to say that the aforementioned solicitors would be pleased to meet with him in Newcastle to go over and execute the terms of the will at his earliest convenience or at the latest, within one month of the date on the letter. He should contact them for information on documents he would need to bring with him to the meeting. It was just as Robert had said.

The next morning he got up and opened a map of England, finding eventually the Tarset Valley. Next he looked it up on the web finding pictures of open moorland, rolling hills and ridges, some high green fields, forest and sheep, rivers, stone towers like castles, and small villages of slate and stone. It was coming back to him. This was a very different world from that of British Columbia. The more he looked the more he became curious about, entranced might be a better word, with the world he was seeing. He was born into it but never really knew it. Later that day a parcel arrived from Newcastle containing Robert's effects including a book entitled, "The Natural History of Northumberland". Inside he saw that it was from Cynthia. She had written, "To My Dearest Robert with love from Cynthia, Christmas 1969 xxx." He could see from the condition of the cover and pages, it was well used. The fact that he had taken it to hospital with him for his final days said a lot. Also in the package was a set of clothes, a faded blue check flannel shirt, worn brown corduroy trousers, a knitted blue sweater, a much used tweed jacket of uncertain colour, a grey tweed flat cap, a pair of strong brown leather shoes, a fountain pen, notebook, and an old watch.

In the notebook Robert had written passages, and made little drawings, some done in watercolours, concerning the weather, sheep, trees, collie dogs, various wild creatures, rivers including the North Tyne, the Rede, Tarset Burn, and the Coquet, the moors, and his own wood. A little bit like Caspar's own field notes. Without thinking Caspar put Robert's watch on his left wrist. It was a vintage Rolex, something suitable to be out with in all weathers. There was also a large envelope containing photographs. Photos of collie dogs, rams, Robert receiving a trophy at sheepdog trials, older people possibly Caspar's grandparents, and then one of his, Caspar's, own much younger looking parents holding a baby, that must be him. Another photo this time of a young woman smiling. Caspar looked carefully, Cynthia. Could it be her? Caspar had to sit down and take it in, this other world, a whole way of life, oddly familiar, reaching out to him in his living room in Vancouver.

In a few hours he came up with a plan. He would ask the department head for a week's leave from his teaching, the students would have all the necessary readings and assignments. He would travel to Newcastle arriving on the Sunday, see the solicitors, visit the farm, and return the next Sunday to deal with the fall semester and all that it entailed. The head approved his request. Caspar had lots of cred. So he booked his flights, KLM Vancouver to Amsterdam, Amsterdam to Newcastle. Next he phoned Neha and invited her to dinner.

He was still in a mild state of shock following his conversation with Robert who had made a huge impression on him, and clearly his nurses too. He had seemed fully at peace with his situation, sanguine, happy almost.

That night he told Neha everything. She sat back in disbelief. He expressed his remorse about Robert, at not having taken any interest in him and his life and astonishment at the inheritance. Neha listened and told him not to be too hard on himself. People do get separated. She had relatives she hadn't seen for years. After the meal she said, "Cas, I think we need to go home and drink a little."

## 28

Sunday afternoon, a week later he arrived at Newcastle airport. Caspar got himself onto the Metro train to take him into the city centre. From there he walked down to his hotel on Grey Street not far from the River Tyne and its iconic bridge. The next day, a Monday, as arranged, he set off to walk up to the solicitors to meet Mr. Willoughby. Jesmond Chambers was on the fourth floor of an ornate Victorian building overlooking Grey's Monument in what was now, mercifully, a pedestrian precinct. Caspar pulled open one of the large highly polished wood, glass and brass doors and entered a high ceilinged black and white tiled arcade. He could walk up the four floors or take an ancient looking lift encased in a wire mesh cage. He opted for the stairs and found the office. Going in he encountered a high dark wooden counter, somewhat ornate and heavy with patina, acting as a kind of barrier to the main area. He stood there for a moment before a young woman with short blonde hair dressed quite formally in a white shirt and grey slacks stood up and said, "May I help you?"

"Yes, I'm Caspar Ballantyne from Canada. I have a ten o'clock appointment with Mr. Willoughby."

"Ah, yes, Mr. Ballantyne. Mr. Willoughby will be you in a few minutes. Would you like a cup of tea, or coffee?" All spoken in the lilting Geordie accent he was getting used to hearing, with the word "grand" uttered on many occasions, just like his parents' speech in fact, and indeed his own when he started school in Canada.

"No thanks, I'm fine."

"Would you take a seat then. I'll let him know you've arrived."

Caspar looked around at the wood paneled office, heard a little buzz of conversation and laughter among the secretaries, and gazed at the ornate ceiling, fluted columns, leafy capitals, and tall windows with pointed arches. There was a definite feel of the past about it. At that moment a gate opened in the counter and a youngish man smartly dressed in a dark navy blue suit and silver tie walked through. "Mr. Ballantyne, Caspar Ballantyne?" he said smiling, his hand held out, "I'm Patrick Willoughby, how do you do."

Caspar stood up and responded in the Canadian, "Pleased to meet you," as he shook the man's hand.

"You're from Vancouver. My wife's cousin lives there. Married to a Canadian. She seems to like it."

At that, Patrick gestured for Caspar to come with him through to a large corner office with a marble fireplace above which was a portrait of a serious looking man, mullioned windows, and several landscape paintings in antiqued silver and gold frames decorating the walls.

Caspar was impressed. It seemed almost Dickensian. He moved closer to one of the pictures, an oil painting, showing a river amidst trees and distant hills. The title at the bottom was, "North Tyne." Then he saw a name, "Robert Ballantyne."

"These are Robert's works?" he asked, surprised, looking from one to the others.

"Oh yes. Mr. Robert was a very much admired artist."

Caspar stood quiet for a moment, looking around the room.

"My father loved Robert's work. That's him by the way," he said pointing to the portrait above the fireplace. The Duke of Northumberland has several in his private collection. Robert painted his pictures outdoors on the spot you know. But he never exhibited any of his work. He just loved being out there communing with nature."

"But these pictures are very good," said Caspar, unaware of his patronizing tone.

"Yes they are," said Patrick giving him a sidelong glance. "Would you care for tea? Coffee?" asked Patrick.

"Tea would be great, thanks."

"Well Mr. Ballantyne..."

"Please, call me Caspar."

"Caspar then. Please, have a seat," he said, motioning to the chair. "It's a pleasure for me to meet you. Our firm has looked after the Ballantyne family for over a hundred years. We only found out recently that Robert had an heir. We were all very sorry about his passing. My father, while he was alive, had been his solicitor. When they met, which they did on occasion in this office, the scotch would flow and the cigars would be smoked accompanied by much laughter. He was quite an interesting chap, Mr. Robert, very learned. There was nothing he didn't know about Northumberland, the history and nature. He was a big reader. And as you can see, he was quite the artist. He was a poet too you know. The ladies liked him. Of course this was besides running a farm of over twelve hundred sheep. He was quite famous for working the sheep with his collies. He bred them at the farm. It was like they spoke the same language. I've seen him in action. He won many trophies at the trials."

Just then, Patrick seemed to remember the business at hand and said, "I just need to see your birth certificate, and something showing your place of residence and we can sign the forms. It will take a few weeks for the probate and then the place will be yours. If you want to go and see it I can supply you with a set of keys. We should probably keep the old deeds and title here in the safe for you to collect, if you wish, on your next visit. We don't want to risk losing anything. Some of the papers are dated 1789, all written out in fine copperplate, pretty much historical documents."

"That's amazing," said Caspar, "I look forward to seeing them."

"With properties this old there are always some questions regarding boundaries, liens, old animosities, supposed ownership of odds and ends, but we have gone through everything very carefully. There should be no surprises. Sign where marked please. Are you planning to go out to the farm?" asked Patrick.

"If I can. I would like to go tomorrow. I'll book a rental car this afternoon."

"Very good. You have my personal number. Don't hesitate if you have any questions or run into anything baffling. This is Northumberland you know. We can be a bit out of step, so they say. But look, let me give you this map. You can see the farm is marked and note it's located in the National Park, an area you will, I'm sure, come to appreciate. Anyway just head out of Newcastle on the A69 and join the A68 for Jedburgh, Scotland, which goes right through the Park. Turn off left for Bellingham, pronounced 'Bellingjum' around here, then take off on this small road, an old Roman road, into the Tarset valley and follow the arrows. Kindly return the keys to Alice before you set off back to Canada." At that he handed Caspar a heavy bunch of large, old fashioned looking iron keys on a big metal ring.

"Actually I do have a question, said Caspar. Can you tell me anything about Cynthia? It's just that Robert asked me to look after her and she was apparently with him when he died. I did meet her years ago when I was a student but haven't seen her since."

"Yes, this will be Cynthia Oughtershaw, also a beneficiary as per your letter. She's Robert's closest neighbour and long-time friend. She's a lovely old bird. Doesn't suffer fools mind. You are bound to meet her as you must drive through her farm to get to Jupiter."

"I see. Well I do have another question. Would you be willing to be my solicitor?"

"We would be delighted Caspar. Our firm is always pleased to represent the Ballantyne family. We would need a small retainer, Alice will let you know about that."

They shook hands and at that Caspar made his exit down the stairs, and walked out past Waterstones bookstore and the high stone column called Grey's Monument.

He wandered around the city for a while admiring the ornate nineteenth century buildings, and the marvelous classical stone portico of the old Theatre Royal. Then he found himself in a narrow, antiquated pub, having a bar running its length, not far from the River Tyne. There he managed to eat a meat pie and drink two pints of local bitter, which he greatly enjoyed. After that he went back to the hotel and slept for two hours.

## 29

On waking he phoned Neha. No answer. He left her a message, wanting to tell her about the different world he'd suddenly dropped into. Caspar was absorbing a lot already, glimmerings of a way of life he barely remembered. As he explored Newcastle, he started to believe that something sublime was waiting to be discovered.

Next morning, a Tuesday, heading west from Newcastle driving on the left in a compact car with a manual shift, god help him, he was looking to link up with the A68, the main road to Scotland. Once on it he found it was a narrow two-lane road. Soon he was aware of the land, remembering. Sweeping green and rolling moorland with dry stonewalls and hedgerows marking out fields on both sides of the road. He made a mental note to learn more about them. At one point he was held up as a flock of sheep driven by a man on a quad and a couple of black and white border collies were crossing the road. He could hear the farmer's whistled instructions to the dogs as they scarpered around keeping the flock together and moving. He stopped the car and took a breath.

This landscape. It was not like BC's. It was noticeably shaped by centuries of human habitation. Yet he had to admit, it had a kind of spare, austere beauty. In the distance looking slightly northeast he could see the looming hills of the Cheviots up against the Scottish border. Caspar drove on seeing the sign for Bellingham. He turned left off the A68 and travelled two miles as instructed, then turned right onto a narrow very straight road heading into the blue distance. Empty moorland all around apart from sheep busily eating grass. Travelling up ever higher he finally drove left on a curve and crested the hill.

Before him in the golden glow of the morning light a broad expanse of rolling fields and woods stretched into the distance. He stopped the car, stood and took in the view. A scattering of small farms, patches of woodland, large mature broadleaf trees. A terrain much layered with time and history. Caspar was not used to it. He carried on a few miles before stopping at a cattle grid just left of the road and a white printed sign saying, "Ravensburn Farm," and underneath, "Jupiter Farm."

Caspar drove down a narrow graveled track turning onto a little wooden bridge crossing a small flowing river, more of a big creek in Canadian terms. This was, he learned later, the Tarset Burn. Carrying on a stretch, the road very bumpy and potholed, he noticed a track veering off left with a wooden sign saying "Ravensburn." He thought he should pay his respects. He turned and drove for a few minutes before encountering a dry stonewall and gate. He got out of the car to the sound of dogs barking. Hell. He'd always been a bit nervous of dogs. Then a voice sharp, commanding, "Rede, Mollie, come." He saw them now, two collies trotting back to a woman in a pinafore, erect, blondish grey hair on her shoulders, sharp looking, in wellington boots and now heading towards him.

"Good morning," called out Caspar.

"Can I help you," came the reply unsmiling, not friendly, not unfriendly, just straight, hands on hips.

"Yes, Mrs. Oughtershaw, Cynthia? I'm Caspar Ballantyne from Canada, I've come to see the farm." At that she stopped and raised her hand to shield her eyes. She gave him a long look up and down before saying, "Goodness me, it is you. Well, you'd better come in."

She opened the gate and he drove on through to the front of a large old house, a door open on the right hand side. She ushered him into a rambling kitchen having a long unvarnished pine table with turned legs and matching chairs. The ceiling seemed quite low and had supporting blackened oak beams running across it. Against the wall facing the door was a large Aga stove giving out some heat. On the wall were a couple of now familiar looking paintings and a large calendar showing a tractor. "A lot of water's gone under bridge eh Caspar? How long has it been?" She looked at him. "I remember your last visit. My goodness, we were still kids. Would you like some tea?"

"That would be nice, Cynthia." So saying, intuiting something, he walked over to her and, unusual for him, put his arms around her, hearing a muffled sob, her face pressed into his shoulder. "Oh, you are so like him," she whispered. "I miss him already." She wiped her eyes and went to the stove.

Cynthia was a striking looking woman in her late sixties, her features now softened by the tears and her recognition of Caspar. She had exchanged the rubber boots for a pair of house slippers. The dogs came in and each got into their own basket by the stove. She moved with the ease of someone still comfortable in her body, which gets rarer with age as things stiffen up. The tea things were placed on the table. "Please Caspar, have a seat. Oh it's so good you've come."

They both sat down and she poured the tea, and slid the biscuits towards him. Then she sat back and gave him a good look. "You know, Robert spoke of you. He said you were a professor, a very clever chap. And I must say, you look very like Robert. I have a picture of him if you would like to see? It's quite recent."

Caspar nodded.

Cynthia handed him a small silver picture frame. The photograph showed Robert in a flat cap, wearing a light tweed jacket and an open necked white shirt. He was holding a collie puppy.

"That's Rede, him in the basket over there taken two years ago."

"Reed is an odd name for a dog."

"Well, it's R-e-d-e not the plant, named after the river in the next valley."

Caspar could see himself looking back out of the picture. Robert, still a vital looking guy though he must have been into late seventies, bronzed and healthy from an outdoor life. Caspar was wishing he could have known him.

"You've known Robert a long time."

"Oh yes, Robert and I were born on these farms, as you were yourself. His father, William, being the eldest, inherited Jupiter. Robert must have been about nine or ten. They were living in the cottage. This must have been around the time you went off to Canada. My husband and I ran this place until he died suddenly ten years ago. Robert and I were children together. He knew so much about nature, and was a marvelous artist, as you can see," as she waved her hand at the framed pictures. "We were a comfort to each other." So saying she cast her eyes down for a moment. "It's not the same without him."

The kitchen fell silent. Caspar said nothing. Then Cynthia stood up and said, "You'll be wanting to get on," and started clearing the table.

"Yes, thanks, I think I'd better."

"Here I'll give you my number. Oughtershaw, that's my married name, Thompson is my maiden name. She handed him a slip of paper.

"It's been lovely seeing you again Cynthia."

She came over and held both his hands. "I hope you will come and see me soon." Then, a little hug. "You feel like him," she said. "Give me a shout if you run into any problems over there. Robert left everything pretty ship shape."

# 30

At that Caspar went back to the car. After a few minutes of driving he could see the stone farmhouse in the distance. It had a slate gable end roof, two chimneys, and a front door in between two large sash windows with four windows upstairs. On the right of the house next to a gate he noticed a mature sycamore tree looking very fine. Soon he was driving through the gate and pulling around left to the back of the house. It was funny. He was beginning to feel like he was putting on some comfortable old clothes. He parked and got the keys.

Standing by the car he looked around, breathing in the fresh air that was, he now noticed, perfumed by an occasional whiff of wood-smoke. There were several low outbuildings, and a small cottage far to the right against the fence. This was where Robert's family had lived when they were kids. Up behind the main house was a barn-like building with double doors. He remembered now. He had lived in the big farmhouse with his mom and dad and grandparents, Archie and Margaret. He'd grown up in Canada without grandparents from either side. Quite a loss now he came to think about it. There were many trees in leaf still and he could see over to the left the orchard with trees in fruit but looking to him a bit forlorn and untended, or was it his imagination? Directly behind the house some distance away over a fence was a sizeable wood. He would have to get in there. Walking further round the back of the house, over towards the corner he could see the back door, heavy, oak, weathered, possibly original.

Caspar found a large iron key on the ring and guided it into a well-oiled lock, which had to be handmade giving over two hundred years of service, imagine. It turned smoothly and he pushed open the door. He stepped inside and onto flagstones, green wellingtons by the door, caps, and coats on hooks, and a long curved handled shepherd's walking stick leaning in a corner. There were thick black wooden beams supporting the ceiling, like at Cynthia's. Caspar stood for a moment sensations rushing back into him. The smell suddenly familiar: things organic and smoky, animals, and the house itself, ingrained by years of life. He noticed the stairs and remembered suddenly going up to bed with grandma Maggie in his blue striped flannel pyjamas carrying his teddy. What a thing is the human mind.

Windows facing big trees rustling in the breeze, roses outside the window, walls three feet thick painted white, flower print curtains, a tall bookcase stuffed with books and papers, Robert's paintings all around, black and white photographs, a desk and of all things, an old computer. It was a narrow room but quite long. On another table he saw a wooden box, paint stained, and with a clutch of brushes lying at the side. Caspar felt as if he were trespassing into a person's inner sanctum.

Looking to the left of the backdoor there was a stone entranceway quite low. He went through and came into a large kitchen also having stone floors. An old Raeburn stove stood inside what was the fireplace. There was another big pine table with turned legs and chairs, all handmade presumably, similar to Cynthia's. A sink and kitchen cabinets were next to a window facing to the back of the house where he had parked the car. More beams across the ceiling he noticed with more paintings and photographs. He felt sure the owner would come back at any moment. The house still had a warmth and life about it.

Caspar turned back away from the windows and went through into a little hallway walking now on worn floorboards leading to the front door. He saw a lawn and flowers, wall and gate, and over the wall an open field and sheep. None belonging to the farm anymore. To the right was a large living room. He went in and felt as if he had gone back in time. Ceiling beams, two large bookcases completely filled, a fireplace with logs stacked at the side, a flaking silver mirror above, an old red

Persian carpet, two large sofas with faded red floral covers like at home, very worn, ones to really sink into, and an armchair, standing lamps, a low square table, piled with books and a bottle of scotch, white discolored walls, and he noticed, a pipe, penknife, box of Swan Vestas matches and tobacco on a window ledge.

In a moment, he picked up the pipe, scraped it out, stuffed in some tobacco and lit it. Then he went in search of a glass, came back and poured himself two fingers of scotch. Sinking down onto one of the sofas, he sat back, and closed his eyes. An eighteenth-century sitting room. Somewhat incredible for one such as he used to the modernity of Vancouver. He took a puff, blew it out, and swallowed some scotch. Good stuff, single malt. As he sat there a feeling of peace came over him. He lingered until his drink and pipe were finished then slid onto his side and fell asleep.

Later on, putting his head around the door of the second front room he discovered a more formal dining room: table and chairs, a sideboard, probably walnut, and a china cabinet filled with antique pieces. Years old he imagined.

Driving back to Newcastle he came to a decision. He would check out of the hotel the next morning, make a deal with the car rental people to keep the car until the Sunday and drop it at the airport. He would stay at the farm for the next four nights. It was just too much to take in otherwise, plus in honesty he couldn't stay away. He tried Neha again but no luck, leaving a brief message. That night he telephoned Cynthia and told her he was coming back. She sounded pleased and invited him to come round for tea, meaning supper at five o'clock. So he went to sleep.

# 31

Early Wednesday morning and he was back on the road. He would stop in Bellingham for some groceries. Soon he was driving down the track past Cynthia's. Caspar tooted the horn. He opened the gate to Jupiter, swung in past the big tree, a sycamore, and parked round by the back door. Once inside the house he looked for the heat and hot water switches and got both going then put the kettle on and made tea. Sitting with his cup at the big old kitchen table, taking it in. Thinking of all the comings and goings in this kitchen, the good news and bad. Drama. Celebrations. Lives lived with sheep and dogs. Weather, seasons, putting the rams or tups to the ewes with the dye bags on their chests, leaving a stain on the ewe's back to show she had been serviced, shearing, dipping, lambing, markets. This much he knew.

There was a big stone cellar full of old Life of Northumbria magazines, a wooden barrel, which turned out to contain still drinkable beer, several cases of wine and scotch, an old bolt-action Lee Enfield army rifle, a bayonet on a shelf, masses of things indistinguishable at the moment, a furnace and large boiler for central heating and hot water he presumed, and boxes piled up. Upstairs he went into four bedrooms all wallpapered with flower prints, beds with shiny satiny eiderdowns, wooden floors and old rugs. He looked in closets and drawers full of clothes, diaries, books, bracelets, pictures, and sepia photos of people he presumed were his ancestors and there was an antiquated bathroom, massive chipped bathtub, long, deep, and narrow, sitting on claw feet, a large ceramic pedestal sink with brass taps and mirror, and a black tiled floor. Later he would come to appreciate the bathtub design in being able to just about fully immerse his entire body in hot water despite the risky business of getting in and out.

Finally he went up a little narrow curving staircase at the end of the hallway to find a small attic door. He switched on the light and went in. Ye gods thought Caspar. There was stuff here from forever. Ladies' crinoline dresses hanging from a rail including an old wedding dress, a top hat and tails, chests, boxes, a picture he pulled from a box containing many was of people smiling in a horse drawn carriage, no end of things going back, he imagined, generations. He would get to it all eventually.

He knelt down and unlatched the lid on a smart, though cobwebby official-looking trunk. Inside to his surprise was a khaki military uniform, a sword in a scabbard--it seemed rusted in--high brown muddied boots, and a pistol in a leather holster. Caspar carefully pulled out the uniform. It was fragile and to his knowledge, a First World War Second Lieutenant's uniform, one star on each of the shoulders. There was a cap with a bronze regimental badge on the front showing "Northumberland Fusiliers" around the circular edge in raised letters and a plume at the top. It had tarnished a dark colour with age. The badge also showed a mounted rider with a spear killing a large serpent-like creature: St. George and the Dragon he assumed. The tunic was spattered with ancient mud and torn. Looking closely he found a burnt hole in the left breast pocket and a dark stain around it that could only have been blood. He unfastened the holster and drew out a rusting revolver. It was still loaded with three cartridges, a black Webley Mark V .455 officer's revolver with the words "War Finish" stamped on the side. Could stop a bus. Delving a little deeper in the trunk he unearthed a bundle of letters tied with string and an official looking envelope. He opened it and found a yellowing certificate that read "The War of 1914-1918... 2nd Lieutenant   P. L. Ballantyne of the 23rd Northumberland Fusiliers killed in action July 1st 1916 leading an attack at La Boiselle during the Battle of the Somme... mentioned in a despatch from Lieutenant-General Sir William

Pulteney…for gallant and distinguished services in the field… his Majesty's high appreciation." This brought a lump to Caspar's throat. Not much for a life. There was also a framed black and white photograph of a young army officer in uniform, must be him: a slight young man with an air of resolve. Putting everything back carefully, he closed the lid. He felt he had disturbed a grave.

Caspar was beginning to realize that there was so much history in this house. A history that he had grown up without but which nevertheless was part of him. Downstairs he found the key on the ring to a long narrow cupboard. Inside was a double-barreled twelve-gauge shotgun and cartridges probably for scaring off foxes trying to get at the hens.

In the kitchen he opened a cream painted cupboard, all the woodwork in the house was cream gloss paint scuffed and yellowed now, inside he found carefully stacked plates, cups and dishes of blue china crockery. He took out a dinner plate, underneath it read Spode Italian c1816 Made in England. Who knew when this crockery actually came into service? It looked worn. In a big drawer he found ancient tarnished cutlery, bone handled dinner knives, nickel plated forks and spoons, some quite large, cooking utensils, until recently still in use. Dinners had been eaten off these dishes and with this cutlery through generations. He went back into the sitting room sat back on a sofa, tired now, and fell asleep. As he awoke he lay still, feeling the tremors and vibes of the old house. How could he have lived so long without being a part of this?

At five o'clock he drove over to Cynthia's. She welcomed him in and offered him a drink. She had shed the pinafore for a nice red frock with long sleeves, the top two buttons open at the neck, cut to below the knee, and had done up her silvery blonde hair in a chignon, reminding him of Neha, and she wore an exquisite but light perfume. Caspar thought he saw a trace of lipstick. She looked attractive thought Caspar as he remembered the strangely compelling blonde haired girl he first knew. How amazing it is to have the chance to see people again from our youth when all our nerve endings are alight. There must be a universal longing for that. Where is a certain person now? What does she look like? What happened in her life? He often had such thoughts of late.

"How are you getting on Caspar?" she asked sipping her glass of wine. Caspar had opted for white wine too, deciding he'd been chancing it a bit of late.

"Pretty good, but there is so much to take in. Things are a bit of a blur just now Cynthia. I was wondering, would you be able to walk over the property with me, tomorrow or the day after, and give me some bearings as to what I'm seeing?"

"I'd be glad to. The day after tomorrow, Friday, would be best for me. First thing. Oh, and while you're visiting you can come over for tea if you like."

"If you're sure, that would be great. By the way, Cynthia, I opened a trunk containing a soldier's uniform in the attic. Do you know anything about it?"

"Well," a pause, "let me think. If I've got this right, the uniform must have belonged to Philip Ballantyne, your great uncle, the brother of your grandfather. He was killed on the Somme in 1916 with the Fusiliers, when he was nineteen. Shot through the lung leading an attack across no man's land. They managed to get him back that night while he was still alive but he died shortly after. The regiment sent his effects back to his parents, your great grandparents, in the very same trunk that he took to the Front. He had, by all accounts, an artistic temperament, a gentle child, always out drawing. It seems to run in the family and he was quite academic. As I remember, from what Robert told me, they sent him to a small school in an old country house near Bellingham. He was going to go to university but then he was called up. You might find some of his drawings in the attic. As you can imagine, the family were devastated. He's buried in a military cemetery in France. His elder brother Lionel came back unscathed."

"How very sad, though I'm glad finally to be learning about the family history. I feel as if Robert has given me a marvelous gift and I don't just mean the farm. I realize now that I know little or nothing about my dad's experiences in the Second World War."

"You could very well find letters from him to your grandmother. He had a heck of a time in Italy what with the hard winter slog in the mountains and being wounded."

Caspar didn't say anything but he felt somewhat abashed, Cynthia seeming to know more about his father's hardships than he did himself.

Anyway, at that, they sat down to a plate of Cynthia's roast lamb followed by apple crumble and custard, which Caspar relished.

"Oh and Cynthia, I wanted to ask you, Jupiter is a strange name for a farm isn't it?"

"Well, it is I suppose, but I'm used to it. Nobody knows its origins for certain but eons ago, so they say, one of your ancestors who was quite an eccentric turned up a piece of a stone tablet in one of the fields. Roman as it turned out, with a fragment of an inscription mentioning the god Jupiter. I know, quite fantastic really, if it even happened. Anyway the farm has been known as Jupiter from that point on, and certainly for all of my life. Nobody thinks about it. At least it's a nice story."

"Amazing but I must say I like the name very much."

# 32

Thursday morning, after a great sleep, Caspar went out to look around the outbuildings and the cottage. He found a stable with a divided door full of stacked logs and in another stable, also with a divided front door, leather harnesses and bridles, a small forge and an anvil with tools, and two saddles. Next door in a large room with double doors opening at the back, he noticed sheep shearing shears, veterinary medicines and washes for ticks and other insects, a pair of cracked leather riding boots, and a derelict looking red Massey Ferguson tractor of unknown vintage.

Then to his utter delight, in the last building he found an immaculate looking pale green four-door Land Rover. He walked around it, opened the driver's door, looked around, and climbed in noticing the simple layout of instruments, gear stick, lever for changing gear ratios, handbrake, and most of all the ingrained smell of wet animal and diesel. In the glove compartment he found an owner's manual dated 1980. The keys were in the ignition, the gear stick in neutral. He turned the key and the engine started straight off. Finding reverse, he released the brake, backed out and drove slowly around the yard. He imagined himself exploring Northumberland, going on expeditions. He felt a tingling sensation at the nape of his neck.

By the end of the day he had been in the second cottage and had a look round. It was smaller than the farmhouse, with two bedrooms, but built at the same time, and still fully furnished. It was a fine building of stone and oak.

Cynthia and he had dinner together that evening and, still feeling jet-lagged, he bade her an early good night.

The next day, Friday, she escorted him around the land closest to the house. First through the fifty or so acres of mainly

Scots Pine and oak, which had not been cut for many decades, nor poisoned with weed killers. Robert, she told him only ever used trimmings and deadfall for firewood. The place was a nature sanctuary filled with plants, flowers, and a myriad of small birds and creatures including the, by now, very rare red squirrel. On they trekked through the orchard of Victoria plum, Lapin cherry, William pear and Cox's Orange Pippin apple trees, all pointed out by Cynthia. Looking over the now empty hen house and wire netting enclosure, Cynthia explained that the cockerel and hens, if he were to have any, could run free during the day but must be in the hen house at night or they would be taken by foxes. She showed him Robert's vegetable garden and at the front of the house, the lawn and roses. Then they went on a walk across the fields nearby where previously the sheep had roamed. Fifteen hundred acres would take much more time to explore.

Caspar was considering a drive out on Saturday around the local countryside and villages. Cynthia accepted his invitation to come along and said she would pack some food and drink. Back in the farmhouse he phoned and got Patrick's approval to leave the keys with Cynthia.

Meeting up the following day Cynthia suggested she do the driving so he could look through the car windows as they travelled around. She took him deeper into the Tarset valley stopping off to look at Greenhaugh, a small village with an ancient pub. Then on to Bellingham crossing a stone bridge over the North Tyne River. Everywhere was rolling moorland, green fields, small lakes, and gushing streams that Cynthia called "burns," large leafy trees forming tunnels over the narrow roads. Caspar was spellbound. It did not have the glorious untouched wildness and sublime mountain vastness of British Columbia, nevertheless it had its own sweeping beauty, denser somehow, more compressed given the scale in space and time.

They crossed the A68 and drove towards Rothbury, an historic town, stone built, quiet and unhurried astride the Coquet

River, then going on to see more rivers and the nature and shape of the land. He noticed again the miles of hedgerows and asked Cynthia to stop and got out to explore. In a fifty yard stretch he was able to identify hawthorn, hazelnut, blackthorn, crab apple, ash, oak, wild pear, sloe, rowan, and noted many smaller plants and flowers. Later he learned that hedgerows, many of which were planted at the time of the enclosures of the 17th and 18th centuries and some going back a thousand years served as boundaries to fields, providing habitat for hedgehogs, mice, stoats and weasels, birds and insects, and secure pathways for badgers and foxes not wanting to cross a field in the open. Hedge laying was really a craft whereby the plants would be partially cut and woven together to grow into an impenetrable barrier. He had seen nothing like it back home. He was also quietly amazed and delighted by the rural simplicity of the hand built, sculpturally interlocking dry stonewalls that marked out the land, running for miles, separating farms, securing flocks of sheep, providing shelter in inclement weather and even habitat for small creatures. Some, harkening back to medieval times, climbed up the sides of very steep and high hills. Imagine, he thought, building one without modern equipment. Another few miles in the car and they would have been on the North Sea coast.

On the way back Cynthia stopped in the village of Elsdon and took him on a walk someway into the hills. They walked through a large broadleaf tree plantation put in to help rebuild the Northumberland forests. She told him about the attacks over the centuries by Border Reivers from Scotland, taking away cattle and people as the reason for all the fortified houses she called "bastles" pointing to the one down the valley in Elsdon. She told him about Hadrian's Wall, and various forts and roads throughout the county. Cynthia pointed to Gallows Hill, on the horizon, leaving the rest to his imagination. That evening as they ate together he told her how much he had enjoyed his visit, getting to know her, thanking her for her hospitality. "I don't know what I would have done without you," he said.

"Oh it was nothing Robert," she said, her eyes moist.

Caspar said nothing and gave her a hug, as she said, "I loved him you know."

"I kind of guessed you did," said Caspar.

"Even as children. But Robert wasn't going to get married. He wanted to be free to work the farm and wander the hills with his paints and all. So eventually I met Michael, and I wanted children, and so…we had a good life together. When Michael died ten years ago Robert and I just seemed naturally to become closer. Amazing isn't it how the heart works." At that her eyes welled up. "It will take me a while to let him go."

After a silence, Caspar said, "Cynthia, I'll be back after Christmas for longer next time. Give me a chance to get a better feel of the place. By the way, I found the Land Rover. I can't wait to get it on the road. Next time. Oh, and one thing, may I leave the keys with you in the morning? Patrick Willoughby says it's ok. I'll be on the road at about 6.30am. I could drop them off, or leave them by the door."

"No, I 'll be up just tap on the door."

"Fine then, see you tomorrow."

At that Caspar gave her a parting hug, went back to the farm and packed. He wrapped up one of Robert's pictures showing the farm and surrounding hills to take with him. He smoked the pipe and had a small farewell scotch sitting on a sofa in the living room. It had been an amazing week. Lying in bed that night he gazed at the flaking ceiling and through the window at the dark outline of trees, the stars, the light of the moon flickering through the clouds and trees on the bedroom walls. There was an old chest of drawers in the room, everything was old, a large wardrobe filled with Robert's clothes and possessions and a bedside table with a small shaded lamp. The bed was high and old fashioned with an iron and brass frame with knobs on, but he was very comfortable. He heard an owl and for a moment was

144

back at Naramata. He had loved the whole aesthetic of the farm, its history, living again in the house of his birth, the paintings, the reality and nature of Northumberland, not forgetting Cynthia. He had enjoyed meeting her again, despite the circumstances, after what, almost half a century. An attractive, intelligent woman, she had been very generous with him. Thinking of his flight, he was mentally crossing the ocean ready to pick up his life at home, see Neha, and get back to his class.

# 33

Cy and Veronica were lying close together in bed in Cy's studio apartment. They had spent the night together which they had been doing more of lately. They were getting along well. Taking walks, having coffee, nothing too extravagant. And they were talking to each other at length about their work. Out of nowhere, she wondered aloud in her distinctive tones, whether for him she was too much like a boy with her trim body and small breasts. Cy was taken aback at her forthrightness. It had never occurred to him. He found her marvelous just as she was. Veronica loved her time with Cy. Her cowboy. He was exotic for her and she wore her cowboy boots everywhere.

But she was taking care to keep some detachment. She had many things to accomplish, and she had to live up to her parents' expectations. Nothing could get in the way, certainly not love. Though she did yearn for more of him, to dissolve fully into their relationship, let it go where it would. Cy loved looking at her, at her diminutive body, her long black hair, and her dark eyes especially. Hearing her little animal sounds as they made love. Her kisses. He wanted to call her "Meifeng." Once alone he swore out loud.

They had been talking about the Dean's plan to remove the aesthetics and ancient history programs. They felt as if their lives, and the lives of others would be irredeemably diminished by the plan. For them their work was a refuge in an age where money ruled above everything. There was a beauty in the work that drew them in, gave them protection from the world's blunt nosed instrumental zeitgeist. How, after all, was one supposed to live in this age if one did not acquiesce to the empty promises of mass marketing, and the facile intrusions of electronic media? For these young people who got it, got the fraud, got the narrowing of lives and despoiling of the planet, there had to be another way, and for them this was answered by being able to engage with thoughts and ideas that first did no harm, and second had intrinsic value. They could appreciate their intellectual journeys, each in their own way, living in the moment. Becoming more complex as whole persons. At the same time, they were arming themselves with ways of thinking and feeling that might not only see them through their own lives in greater fulfillment, but also contribute to the common good.

# 34

Now back in Canada, Caspar was launched straight back into his teaching and he had Veronica and Cy to see for an update on theses progress. He also had to work on the photographs for the December exhibition. In amongst all of these matters, thoughts of Northumberland rippled through him and Robert's pictures. The one he had brought back with him now on his living room wall entitled "Jupiter." It was superbly good. He resonated with it after his visit. The work had soul. He couldn't stop looking at it.

He phoned Neha and invited her over for pizza. They greeted each other with a hug. He told her about his trip. She could see the glow in his eyes. They ate, drank a glass or two of wine, and finished up with a cigarette. "Cas, I've missed you," said Neha.

"I've missed you too Neha." They embraced and kissed, holding on to each other after he'd shown her the picture. Then Caspar said, "I'm going back to Northumberland after Christmas for a couple of months. Would you like to come? It's a completely different world there. Lots of nature. Everything is old and weathered. Everywhere stone and history, rivers, fields and sheep right up against the Scottish border. Neha, I found this trunk in the attic. Belonged to my great uncle Philip. It had in it the uniform he was killed in during the First World War. He was only nineteen, Neha, just a boy. He was going to go to university. My cousin Robert, he was a wonderful artist and sheep farmer. I'm going back in January, after I take care of all of the stuff, you know. Could you come?"

Neha pulled back a bit. Said nothing. Lit another cigarette. "Wow Cas, I've never seen you like this. You seem so taken over by it. I'm glad for you. But, you know, I have to teach and I'm scheduled for a couple of conferences in the spring." Then a puff on her cigarette.

Caspar didn't speak for a while then said, "I get that Neha, of course you'll be very occupied in the New Year. Well I just thought I would see whether it might interest you. May I top you up?"

"Thanks Cas. I'll see what my schedule is like. Maybe I can squeeze in a week in May."

After that they chatted, and Neha left, having an early class.

A week later he received a letter from Patrick Willoughby in Newcastle to tell him that Robert's will had gone through probate and he was now the legal owner of Jupiter Farm. At that he felt a bolt of happiness. He was already at the farm in his mind, starting the Land Rover. Maybe Neha would come around. He was a bit disappointed by her lack of enthusiasm, and as he now thought, her lack of communication while he was away. He didn't really understand it. That night as he lay in bed he was thinking of his last night in the farmhouse in the old bed of Robert's. There was such an atmosphere in that room. A bright moon disappearing in cloud, then flickering on the bedroom wall. He fell asleep and dreamed of the farm. He was with Cynthia, walking across her land with the two dogs Rede and Mollie.

The next morning as Caspar awoke, the dream came back to him. Cynthia. He thought of her in her blue dress and chignon hair and imagined her as she was on the tractor that day during his visit from Cambridge. She'd teased him as being a brainbox, testing him, bright and vital. He saw how she was in sway to Robert without his doing anything. Indifferent almost. Caspar was the dumb kid from the colonies or so he felt. The ambiance was new to him, as he had never been at a loss with girls back home.

Caspar was up to his neck in teaching, attending meetings, giving public lectures, writing, serving as external examiner, reviewing academic articles, attending Faculty meetings, consulting with his grad students, working on his pictures, having a walk or two and being with Neha, by now his most important wish. And yet he was beginning to have the feeling that Neha was content with the way things currently were. Maybe she was right. And he, himself, what did he want? She had been pretty marvelous as a friend. He would have to see whether something deeper might emerge.

One highlight of his week was his visit to a tree in the grounds of a downtown city hospital he was passing on a walk. The tree was planted decades ago from a seed of the tree Hippocrates had taught under on the Greek island of Kos, a Hippocratic Plane Tree, or so a plaque read. Caspar had certain trees he regarded as friends dotted around the West Side.

He photographed them, made notes about them, plotted their street locations. He stood under them silent, appreciating their form and leaf shape, the effects of light filtering through their canopies, their size, health, and the birdlife they attracted. Vancouver supported the growth of a huge variety of conifer and broadleaf trees. It was one of its blessings, increasingly important as the traffic and pollution were intensifying of late.

Caspar thought long and hard on Wittgenstein's famously enigmatic phrase about ethics and aesthetics being one. He had written articles about it. It raises complex philosophical questions, and who really knows what the man meant? Both areas in the practical sense require a measure of disinterestedness, meaning a lack of selfish motivations. How can we show compassion to someone if we are thinking about how we might use them to foster our own purposes or appreciate a work of art if its dollar value is uppermost in our minds?

Goodness and beauty were ends in themselves, difficult to define. Both involve feeling as a guide to judgement. Caspar also believed that when art managed to show the realities of life in its beauty and ugliness, good and evil, then ethics and aesthetics could overlap. Portraiture can show human character. Landscape art brings us closer to the earth and its fragile ecology, indeed one of his students had written a doctoral thesis on this very subject. But they are different in the sense that in life, ethics takes precedence over aesthetics, humanity comes before beauty.

Unawares, Caspar often slipped into thinking of his times with Marjorie. Back in the small hotel in Covent Garden named for an eighteenth century novelist, where they had gone for years. Hours spent in the National Gallery, the Wallace collection and many photography galleries. And they often went to the same places, bookshops, coffee shops, and pubs. They attended many concerts and talks. Caspar liked to visit old buildings, and the newest on the skyline. Walking by the Thames. Being in bed together after a full day in the streets, taking the tube, visiting a park. Just talking. Such memories came of their own accord. Times spent together at the National Gallery in Ottawa and museums in New York, and talks he had given with her accompanying him at various universities in North America. They spoke with warmth of a philosophy conference they had attended in Regina. The dinner put on in a small church hall by local ladies serving rye and ginger ale. A small ceramic cow made by local school kids had been placed by everybody's plate as a gift in honour of Joe Fafard, a Saskatchewan artist.

Sometimes he wished he'd gone with her. Marjorie's uncle Lionel had died a week after his wife, her aunt Iris, had died. They found him in his armchair, a scotch by his side.

But Saturday evening was the Purcell concert. He would take Neha for an early supper before going on to the Vancouver Playhouse, an intimate, comfortable, old-fashioned theatre. The concert was wonderful. They had been enthralled and had sat on for several minutes as people filed out, not yet able to move. Neha stayed over at Caspar's. They had an early night and slept soundly and comfortably together. On Saturday morning they were up early, out to a café on 4th and Trafalgar for breakfast then onto the forest trail following Caspar's map. He had to admit she was game, not ever having been a walker. She had on khaki shorts and boots, with a bright green rainproof shell. They would cover around six miles. Caspar had bought her a stainless water bottle, which she kept in her new daypack, also from him. She seemed quite into it asking him questions, pointing out trees and listening to birdcalls. Caspar explained to her the difference between crows and ravens, the way they looked and the way they sounded. Ravens were bigger than crows, often alone or in pairs, very black and shiny, bluish in the light, with a formidable beak. They stopped later on hearing one. Back that afternoon to Caspar's for a meal, then, on the spur of the moment, out to a movie. They seemed to be grooving along nicely. But he found he didn't say much about Jupiter for some reason.

The next day he did his class preparation, marked essays, then worked on his photographs. The idea of Rivers and Streams was coming together, a different take on landscape. He remembered each picture, where he was, how he got it, the feeling at the time. He would have to give the curator the pictures and an artist's statement by the end of November. One of his favorites was the picture of the large green toad that swam by him in the Okanagan River. The toad was quite sharp in focus, shown from slightly above and to one side as it was starting a dive just under Caspar, legs outstretched, webbed feet outlined, eyes open, riverbed plants streaming out in the current. He was starting to think this would be one of his best bodies of work. Interesting how creative growth can still occur after years of doing the same subject. This is what kept him coming back.

# 35

It was getting towards the end of October. Caspar was meeting with Veronica. She had completed four out of the five chapters in draft and was well into the final chapter. So she was doing well. Cy was roughly the same. He told them both to submit the drafts to him before anyone else. He would advise on edits and if necessary, read second copies before giving anything to the second members. They were expected to give him as close to ready-to-defend versions that they could by the end of November. Also, he had arranged to see Shirley in the coming week.

The agenda for the Senate meeting set for mid-November was published. Caspar didn't know what Shirley would do in the meeting. Nor did he feel he should try to force something out of her. She had her own survival to think about. He decided to arrange a meeting with Philippa and try to get a sense of her position. What had made her undertake the Dean's prerogative maneuver?

If anything Caspar would have expected her, as a literature person, to go out to bat for ancient history and aesthetics. On the Friday following his morning class he arrived at the Dean's office. She was waiting for him. "Hi Caspar. Come in please take a seat. I can guess what you want to see me about."

"Hi Philippa, how are you? Yes well you would be right. Tell me if you wouldn't mind why you felt it necessary to just axe our programs yourself, no discussion? Not that I'm averse to decision-making from the top, god knows you have so little authority as it is, and a difficult job to do with a bunch of prima donnas but I just thought we, Ronnie and I, deserved more than that. Our programs are, as you know, if we must use this language, leaders in the field. We get the top students. Ronnie and I have good reputations academically. I can see the need possibly to diversify our offerings, given the state of things, but surely we don't have to kill off highly valued programs in the process. Philippa, you know as I do that the University is renowned for its liberal emphasis, which in the view of many is more required than ever. Are we to become like everybody else? All business and technology?" At that Caspar took a breath. The Dean, he realised, was no longer listening.

"Casper, I'm sorry but we must start moving forward with our modernization." Her face was blank, expressionless. He felt she was looking at him without really seeing him. "And I had to act quickly to secure the Foundation grant. I'm sorry for your situation but I have to work for the overall good."

Caspar looked at her almost sympathetically. "Philippa," he said quietly, "I think I have an idea of your situation here but somebody has to hold the line on behalf of the University. I think you know what I mean. Please think about that. And may I say if you took the one million that should fund two faculty positions for the Asia program for at least five years, by which time Ronnie and I could be dust."

"But Caspar, the program changes are needed now as part of the updating process and will help convince the bureaucrats we're serious. I'm sorry but the decision from my office is final." It suddenly dawned on Caspar. Bloody Hell. Pulling his and Ronnie's programs was, obvious to him now, a condition of the grant. Hence Philippa's guilty inability just to talk with him about it. Things were starting to make sense. Adsetts, as was well known, specialized in his real estate business in catering to off-shore clients. And as had recently been revealed in the news, some of these real estate deals were in essence forms of money laundering. Expensive homes bought and left empty. Places to park cash. So was there a connection among Adsetts, the Asian grant, getting a foothold in the university, and the attempt to control Veronica by among other things removing Caspar? It was just too fantastic.

He breathed out slowly. She was working her hands together in her lap. "Well Philippa," he said, "would you at least think things over?" There was so much more he could have said but nothing she didn't already know. So he stood up, wished her well, and left.

# 36

Caspar was called to an appointment a couple of days later to meet with the Chancellor. Formally dressed with tie and jacket, he was trying to stay cool. The secretary ushered him into a large dark wood paneled room overlooking the harbor and north shore coastal mountains and seated him in front of an imposing Victorian desk. Two minutes later, the Chancellor strode in offering his large strong hand, which Caspar took, holding onto it with his own firm grip. "Good morning Dr. Ballantyne, how are you?"

"I'm very well Mr. Chancellor, and you?"

"Great, I'm great Caspar. May I call you Caspar?"

"Sure."

"Good, well please call me Harry. Look Caspar, to be frank, I know you're unhappy about the program changes, as is Ronnie, and who wouldn't be but you must know it's time to move on. We can't be sure of our funding unless we shift more to business programs and programs on Asia. Just look at our advantageous position on the Pacific Rim and the growing Asian population in the city. Something has to be done, and there's plenty of opportunity for students interested in your and Ronnie's areas out at Victoria U. So I ask you to support these changes. You could pick up other courses. You wouldn't have to retire until you are ready. There would probably be an opportunity for you in the Foundation, someone with your qualifications and experience. What do you say?" Adsetts sat back in his big chair with the air of a man ruling his kingdom.

Caspar looked at him square on, unsmiling, "Well, I agree with you about the need for a good program on Asian culture. I support that wholeheartedly."

"Good, good, Caspar, now we're getting somewhere," said the Chancellor.

Caspar had many friends and colleagues in different institutions across China. They were warm, kind and sincere. He'd had many wonderful experiences with them, and he had learned a lot. The standard in the Art Institutes was amazing. For dedication, skill and sheer ability nothing in the west came close. It was the Chinese state, the Party and oligarchs he had trouble with. The dictatorship. Things were getting heavy.

"But, not to be left in your hands under the influence of your associates" said Caspar, now face to face with Adsetts, "You really have no remit to get involved in academic matters. I think in the right hands, the Asia program could be really good, and needed. But you must keep your hands off it. It can be nobody's political tool." Then he calmly and steadily said, "I know what you are up to Adsetts with the grant." Then a silence. Another pause, then with some force, "You tell your friends to leave my student alone. You should be supporting her. You should be proud of her." Both men were now standing. Caspar 's face, set like granite, was just inches from the Chancellor's. "You bastard. How could you do this? You're a traitor and you are shaming your position. One way or another it will all come out. I will make sure of it."

Adsetts stood up, no longer smiling, and said, "Look Caspar, this is all very upsetting. I don't want a fight with you but you have annoyed some powerful people. And there could be repercussions. You must know that. Do you really want all this trouble at your age? Couldn't we come to some agreement for everyone's benefit?"

Caspar looked him in the eye for a moment wanting to punch him, before saying, "There's no chance of that. There is no 'everyone's benefit.' But you can't see that. And you can tell your friends what I've said." Then he turned and left the office, walking across the academic quadrangle, breathing in the sea air glad to be feeling he had drawn the line.

He telephoned Shirley and let her know the situation. One thing that bothered Caspar though, after he had ended his phone call, was whether the University should be taking money at all from this Foundation. It was asking for trouble in his mind. Caspar now knew who they were dealing with. But what was their long game? You don't know what damage might be done, just by letting them in. But what could he do about that? How could you argue against accepting a million bucks without being accused of sour grapes or other malign motivations?

# 37

A week before the Senate meeting set for November 15th Caspar received a letter from the Journal of Environmental Aesthetics letting him know that London University had given him the prestigious Richard Wollheim Prize for the best article in aesthetics for the year. Caspar was pleased. This was significant international recognition for the direction of his work, important for his students particularly in the upcoming doctoral defences, and especially for the aesthetics programme. He was ahead of the game for once.

Neha phoned him later that afternoon. They arranged to meet at her apartment. He gave her a brief run down on the day's events including news of the award. Neha came over, put her arms around him and said she was proud of him and she loved him. He kissed her and said, "I love you too. You have been a wonderful friend and support to me. I never thought I could ever feel like this again and it's all due to you. You are so beautiful. You know I'm going to retire soon. I want to see more of you. We can get out into the woods and seashore together. Have you spent much time in the Gulf Islands? Did you know they are almost all named after Spanish ships coming up from Mexico in the eighteenth century? On Saturna Island you can watch pods of killer whales hunting salmon barely offshore. Right off the eastern tip is a sea lion colony. You can fish for rock cod. The ocean is dark green and deep. I want us to go there. The island is small and quiet. We can hike and swim. The Salish people went there in the summer to fish." Caspar paused for breath.

"Sounds wonderful Cas and I want to come with you but I'm so busy with my work. Can you give me a bit more time?"

"Take all the time you want, of course. You have your own life. I have no desire to take you away from that. We both have our interests and long may they flourish." With that he kissed her on the cheek and went to get his pipe.

During the next few days Caspar was thinking through his approach for the Senate meeting. He didn't want to hurt Shirley or Philippa. They were both in their own ways stuck in a hard place. Shirley was inevitably part of the curriculum reform process. You could say she was leading it. Philippa too was an officer in the administration and on one level it made sense to cut aesthetics and ancient history in order to update the curriculum. Who could fault anyone for pushing for change in the current climate. The Asia Studies proposal, would, he felt, pass easily. He wouldn't fight it. It was needed. Nor did he want to fight the aesthetics and ancient history withdrawal motions on the heels of a defeat. But he now knew, or suspected, some untoward persuasion had been applied and he was definitely not happy with the use of the so-called Dean's prerogative. It was, however, still legal and de facto, and indeed, as he now thought, in some way payback for Veronica. Ronnie unfortunately was being drawn in because the same change arguments applied to his subject and drew away suspicions of political malfeasance towards aesthetics.

On another front, letters from England started to arrive. There were bills for the farm, and the solicitor's final account, which was to be paid from the estate. There would be some cash left, a couple of thousand pounds, which Patrick would hold for instructions. He had a card from Cynthia asking after him. Looking forward to seeing him. She told him all was well at Jupiter. One big thing Caspar began to think about was that he knew he would never be able to keep three properties running on his pension, nor did he want to particularly. But as things stood he loved his Okanagan cottage and was irresistibly pulled by the farm.

# 38

Tuesday November 15th, six-thirty pm. Caspar, wearing his old black and scarlet doctoral gown from Cambridge University, with tweed jacket, white shirt and tie underneath, was on his way to the Senate Chamber, possibly the oldest piece of architecture in the University. The interior was famous. Shaped like a small Roman amphitheatre inside, original, if somewhat battered, Douglas Fir seats and desks built in a wide arc tiered downwards to a smaller arc on the bottom row. Microphones had been fitted at each seat as well as web connections. In the middle of the well-lit podium, a large ornate oak desk and three chairs occupied the centre area having been used by every president since the beginning. Circling around, at the top, a visitors' gallery gave space for fifty or so guests. The chamber itself had seating for around one hundred and fifty. So it was small and a little awe-inspiring. Crystal chandeliers hung down from a dome of a ceiling that had a stained glass circular skylight at the top.

Caspar saw from a distance a gathering of people around the entrance. He spotted Cy and Veronica. They waved and came over. "Hello Dr. Ballantyne," said Cy," giving the gown a look over. "Good luck in there." Veronica grasped both her hands together, Chinese style, and shook them looking at Caspar. He thanked them for their support.

A few students from the ancient history program were standing talking with Ronnie, who was wearing his scarlet and black doctoral gown from the University of Toronto. Great minds think alike thought Caspar.

They greeted each other and shook hands firmly. Then Ronnie and he walked together through a stone archway and along a gothic stone corridor with a mosaic-tiled floor and into the chamber itself. People were talking in whispers and hushed tones, looking around and nodding to each other at the sight of Caspar and Ronnie in their formal attire. They chose seats at the back designated for guests who had interests in the meeting. Caspar noticed the students were taking their seats in the gallery. It was already close to full. Now at a minute to seven the doors were closed.

Shirley, wearing her crimson academic gown from Harvard, her Academic Vice-President, Dr. Simon Wong, and the President's personal assistant Vicki Flynn, entered from the side accompanied by the Chancellor, Harry Adsetts, dressed smartly in a dark business suit and tie with a black gown on top. Caspar and Ronnie looked at each other. Something was definitely up. There was more whispering among the senators. Shirley exchanged a word or two with people seated on the front row then moved to the desk and sat down. Dr. Simon Wong was on her right, Vicki on her left. Harry Adsetts sat on the front row facing the President's desk. At seven o'clock precisely she raised her gavel and with a crack declared the meeting started. She welcomed the Chancellor as a guest of the meeting.

For the first fifteen minutes or so the agenda was examined, fussed over, and accepted. Minutes were declared free from errors, points addressed and so on until Shirley read out "New Business. Item One. We have a motion from the Faculty of Humanities, details of which have been circulated and are in your agenda documents. Dr. Lindstrom, would you like to introduce the motion?"

The Dean of Humanities, not in academic dress, but very smart in a blue business suit stood up in the first row over on the President's left and in a firm clear voice said, "Yes thank you Madam Chair I would. This new Asia Studies program is funded by a start up grant of one million dollars from the Pacific Rim Foundation for which we are very grateful, and it is needed to address a marked gap in our program offerings. It is essential we fill that gap because of our geography as a Pacific Rim country, second because of the changing geo-political order in the world, third, to broaden our range of study given the multicultural make up of our society, fourth, to foster recruitment from a broader ethnic and cultural population in our province, across Canada, and around the world, fifth to modernise our university in order to meet the changing needs of the economy…" And on she spoke for several more minutes.

Shirley then asked, "Dr. Lindstrom, are you ready to make the motion?"

Again in a firm voice Philippa read, "I move the addition of the undergraduate program of 'Asia Studies' into the Calendar for the Faculty of Humanities."

Shirley thanked her and asked for a seconder. A hand went up from the person sitting next to Philippa. "Seconded by the Associate Dean, Academic, Dr. Sadhana Sadra. Thank you." Shirley turned to the Senate body, thanked the Dean, and asked, "Is there any discussion?"

The chamber sat silent. People knew when to keep their mouths closed. Caspar cast a glance at Ronnie and both nodded slightly, saying nothing.

"In that case," said Shirley, "question, all in favour." A throng of hands went up. Vicki Flynn did the counting. "All against." Shirley gave it time, looked around. Nobody moved. Vicki handed her a slip of paper. Then she spoke, "The motion is passed unanimously." There was a bit of turning around including the Chancellor, Adsetts, who looked serene from a distance.

"Now we go to Item Two, said Shirley." A pause, then unexpectedly, she said, "For Items Two and Three I will vacate the Chair and hand over to Dr. Simon Wong, Vice-President Academic." With that Shirley went over and sat on the front row to the left of the Chancellor with several seats space between them. Heads were turning and nodding, expressions of surprise were being shared, a little buzz of talk could be heard.

Simon moved to Shirley's seat and intoned, "Thank you Dr. James. Ready Dr. Lindstrom?"

"Thank you, Mr. Chairman," said Philippa, casting a quizzical glance toward Shirley and looking down at her documents. "I would like to make a change and request the meeting's indulgence by combining motions in Items Two and Three, concerning the removal of Ancient History and Aesthetics from the Calendar. These motions are very similar and we could save the meeting some time."

People re-read the motions. Simon then said, "Are there any objections?"

Caspar and Ronnie looked at each other, both shrugged thinking are we stronger together or apart? Again neither wanted to start their responses with an early defeat due to objections so they kept quiet. But they weren't sure what this meant. There being no objections, Simon asked Philippa to introduce the new motion.

Philippa then declared, "I move the withdrawal of the graduate programs in Ancient History and Aesthetics in the Faculty of Humanities from the Calendar."

Simon thanked her then asked, "Is there any discussion?"

At this point Shirley rose to her feet, straightening her gown. She tapped the little portable microphone on her lapel. All eyes were fixed firmly on her. There was absolute silence in the chamber. "Yes, Mr. Chairman," she said, turning towards the Chair. "I would like to argue against this motion." An audible gasp could be heard. Heads were turning, eyebrows raised. This was unusual but permitted procedure. She stood erect in the centre of the podium area looking up and around at all the senators, guests and students, including the Chancellor. Shirley began to speak, clearly and firmly enunciating her words so they echoed throughout the chamber. "Mr. Chairman, Chancellor, senators, members of faculty, students, guests: first, I question the undemocratic nature of the process. Why was it necessary to by-pass the normal Faculty procedures for program withdrawal? This Dean's prerogative rule hasn't been used in decades for a good reason. It excludes members of Faculty from having their legitimate input. Used once it could be used again. Second, I would argue that these programs, ancient history and aesthetics, by focusing on culture, are not redundant. Now more than ever they are needed in an age of increasing emphasis on technology and commerce. A university is more than a cog in the market system. Universities should inspire us to lift our minds and spirits beyond immediate fiscal and pragmatic requirements important as these are. Without an understanding of history and philosophy, especially as these disciplines relate to the origins of the modern world and the arts, we would be diminished as human beings. A university has a responsibility to address the whole person. I would argue that ancient history and aesthetics are both in their ways forms of literature that examine and explore significant events and qualities relevant to us all, and as such are as important as any other subject in the university."

Shirley paused, took a drink from the glass of water on the President's desk, dabbed her mouth with a tissue, then straightened up and faced the chamber. "I have letters here from distinguished professors at Cambridge University in England, the University of Toronto, and Harvard, all writing in support of our programs, which they see as being among the finest in the world. Professors Ballantyne and Ferguson are described as being in the top two or three scholars in their fields internationally. Both have won the highest awards for their work, which gives esteem to our university and respect to our graduates. The loss of these programs would be a tragedy for students and the University's academic reputation. We must strive to keep our programs of excellence, programs that have defined the university and made it distinctive for generations. The questions raised by these programs are as relevant today as they were a century ago." At that she distributed copies of the letters she had mentioned, and quoted a line or two from each as applause and a cheer burst out from the students in the visitor's gallery and a few scattered senators. This was greeted by the striking of the gavel and a warning from the Chair that this not be repeated. At that the President gave a slight nod to the Chair and sat down.

The Chancellor was on his feet immediately, arm raised, indicating he wanted to speak. The Chairman told him he would put him on the speakers' list and reluctantly he sat down.

Ronnie stood up to speak and was greeted with applause from the students. The Chair rose again and gave the gallery a final warning. After salutations, Ronnie argued eloquently for several minutes on the value of ancient history in our understanding of different ways of being human, from pre-history to the medieval world, that have an irreplaceable bearing on who we are today. The old scholar held out both hands and ended his speech with feeling by saying, "By looking deeply into the past, across a broad spectrum of cultures, we stand to appreciate the value and place once held for the arts, poetry, philosophy, myth, story, religion, science and languages across millennia and thus be in a position to understand and evaluate the nature and quality of our own civilization. As such, ancient history has a unique and irreplaceable place in the curriculum, a Latin word meaning course to be run." Ronnie slowly lowered his arms, turned and sat down not moving or speaking.

The Chair then nodded to Harry. He stood up and faced the room. "Let me say as Chancellor, I'm proud of this university and of its academic reputation. But progress is important. It's essential now for us to move forward, to develop new academic areas the government feels are important: technology, finance, commerce and real estate. These are the subjects that will ensure the University's future. Now is the time to cut outmoded and irrelevant subjects with small enrolments that do not foster prosperity. I urge senators to recognize these realities. The Asia Program is a part of the new direction, but resources to support it are scarce and must be culled from programs that are, if anything, an outmoded elitist luxury. I urge you to support the motion." He sat down. People looked around. It was unheard of for a Chancellor to address the Senate in such a partisan way, especially on academic matters. Nevertheless, politics being politics, people were listening.

Dr. Wong signaled to Caspar who stood up and looked around the chamber, as if getting his bearings. Then he began, speaking slowly, "Mr. Chairman, Madame President, Chancellor, senators, colleagues, students, guests: I would first like to echo the sentiments of our President, Dr. James, and my esteemed colleague Dr. Ferguson. This attempt to cancel programs in the Calendar without due and fair consideration by Faculty must be resisted as with any arbitrary exercise of power. It is at worst subject to abuse and at best anti-democratic. I ask senators to think carefully about the Dean's action before casting their votes. But on to philosophy and the question of what aesthetics has to offer to the curriculum. This is not an easy question to answer because concepts and logic will only get us so far in the study of aesthetic theories or indeed in thinking about aesthetics in the lived world. Students quickly realize that analysis, valuable as it is, and necessary, will not yield finite results when it comes to concepts such as beauty, appreciation, imagination, and feeling, or indeed, understanding, which lie at the core of the discipline and one's aesthetic interactions with the world.

I'm glad my colleague Dr. Ferguson used the word 'appreciation' in relation to the subject matter of ancient history because I would like to do the same for my field. Appreciation has become an almost defunct word, given present preoccupations with the market mentality. Who has time for appreciation? What is its cash value? Isn't it elitist? Aesthetics nudges us gently towards matters of intrinsic value through the recognition of perceptual and appreciative awareness. Just to apprehend the being of another, resonate with a poem or piece of music, hold attention onto a butterfly, gaze at a photograph, or a shaft of sunlight coming through a kitchen window, is an engagement in which one's feelings for the qualities of the moment can be heightened. Aesthetics teaches us to love the world through our own experience, not to the exclusion of social or moral ends, but as a dimension that can lift the spirit and help make life worth living. Aesthetics offers the hope that there is more to life than the bottom line. It speaks to the experience of the subjective individual, to the value of the singular voice and style, of imagination, which can be a gesture towards freedom, away from the grip of rules and authority. Aesthetic attention is the opposite of what is being imprinted on young minds by the constant daily emphasis on economics: supply and demand, competition, means/ends thinking, technocracy, and profit. The ineffable encountered in aesthetic experience is a reminder that not everything can be pinned down objectively or made into a saleable algorithm.

Yet, the aesthetic realm is still valued by many, as one sees in the popularity of art exhibitions, concerts, piano lessons, numbers of amateur photographers, home decoration, stamp collecting, gardening, pet ownership, country walks, and arts programs generally, not excluding community classes in ballroom dancing, for example. Attending to things for their own sakes, for their in-built rewards and satisfactions, as millions of amateurs do, is quite a subversive idea when you think about it. And the careful probing study of aesthetic theories from the past and present can educate us about the nature of the arts and more recently, the importance of eco-systems. Environmental aesthetics relies on appreciation to foster preservation. An old growth forest, for example, can be loved for its very qualitative existence, for the joy of being in it, as opposed to its reduction in thinking to so many board feet of lumber.

Aesthetics as a study has its own philosophical methods, which tend to the persuasive rather than the absolute. The aesthetic is a value that underpins instrumental striving. What, you might ask, is all the hard won accumulation supposed to be for? I note the view of Ludwig Wittgenstein to the effect that when all scientific questions have been answered, matters of human life remain untouched, and this latter is the irreplaceable terrain of the humanities of which aesthetics is an integral part. For these reasons aesthetics should be preserved as part of the University curriculum."

Caspar fell silent. The chamber was still and quiet. People were taking it all in. Then, just as the Chair was about to move on to another speaker, Caspar, who had not sat down, spoke up. "Mr. Chairman, I am not quite finished. May I take a few more moments? "

"The Chair recognizes Dr. Ballantyne."

"Thank you. Mr. Chairman. I'm pleased the University has received such generous funding from the Foundation to support the new program as just approved. Yet I do wonder about the source of such funding, and whether it is necessary to remove our programs in order to facilitate the new one. I have it on good authority that the relatively meagre teaching resources such as we have in aesthetics and ancient history, are not needed in light of the grant and current Faculty funding. So the question remains, why cut the programs? It is perfectly reasonable and possible to offer the new and old programs together. Deleting the old programs adds nothing to the rationalization that more programs are needed in technology and business. It could be argued that arts programs are needed not just for what they offer that is unique but also to provide for balance as the curriculum is changed, as the President intimated. Then again, nobody gives away money, especially in such a large amount, without wanting something in return. In this case the strongest contender is to support an agenda. This may be completely benign and a genuine gift, leaving us to design a curriculum and hire suitable instructors. On the other hand, it might be a way to use the University to satisfy external and un-academic aims. In which case our integrity would be at risk."

At this point, Adsetts was half out of his seat, red faced, speaking directly to the Chair in strident tones. Simon silenced him palms outwardly upraised. And signaled him to be seated. This was not something the Chancellor was used to in his normal business life as a CEO, but he had to swallow it.

"Thank you, Mr. Chairman," Caspar continued. "Also I have to ask why the Chancellor felt it necessary to act in such a partisan way, first by getting involved directly with the Foundation to promote the new program on its behalf, the financial backing of which, as I have noted, is not exactly transparent, and second, by arguing before this chamber for the cancellation of existing and highly respected graduate programs? This is most unusual, not to say highly questionable behaviour. Colleagues, academic matters are a Faculty concern, to be argued out in public rather than behind closed doors, let alone by hidden interests or leveraging of authority. The reasonable impression might be given that there are other than purely academic issues at stake. And let me add, the distribution of teaching resources is normally based on legitimate curriculum needs established by due process, and as such, is outside the purview of the Chancellor."

This was a bit of a stretch but Caspar gambled that Adsetts would have more to lose by challenging him openly than remaining silent. And so it was, at least verbally. In any case, Caspar was ready for him. He was here to fight it out.

Adsetts could now be seen vigorously shaking his head and turning to glare up at Caspar raising his hands and shrugging his shoulders.

The previous week Caspar had met with Veronica about a question in her thesis when he raised the matter of the email. Should he say something at Senate. The dilemma was, she felt in response, that if they did nothing it would look weak and this could potentially invite further actions, or if they pushed back in some way this might invite retaliation. Either way she was now of the opinion that she could not return home. On balance she was in favour of doing something. From her experience she thought shining a light would signal they were not going to accept it. Publicity could be their weapon, with more potentially to come. Caspar talked this over with her at length looking at it from different sides before agreeing to speak on the matter at the meeting.

"There is one more issue I would like to address Mr. Chairman, and this concerns the serious matter of academic interference. My student received an email from an offshore source demanding, in a threatening way, that she cease and desist work on her approved PhD dissertation, which it seemed, was not pleasing to certain unknown authorities. Needless to say this was very worrying and an attack on our most cherished value, that of academic freedom. All students at this university from whatever culture or region of the world, are entitled to the same rights and protections namely, unfettered choice and freedom of inquiry within established disciplinary bounds.

I would like to request that our Chancellor, given his many offshore contacts through his real estate interests, as an officer of the University, investigate this matter and ensure such a thing is not repeated. I will put the necessary material into his hands. Then I'm sure he will be as proud as I am of our student who is putting the free search for truth above personal worries. She stands, I believe, as a potent emblem of what this university is all about. She refuses to be intimidated. Every single one of us should stand behind her. I look forward to the Chancellor's timely handling of the matter and his report back to this body of the results of his investigation. Thank you, Mr. Chairman."

At that Caspar sat down, took out a tissue and wiped his brow. There was s silence in the chamber then spontaneous applause from the students and a few senators and guests. Members were conferring animatedly, casting glances at Adsetts, who looked very uncomfortable, exposed and alone in an alien and un-compliant world. This was news to them. What the heck was going on? Simon gave up on controlling the meeting for the time being. He sat down and looked across at the President who had a wry smile on her face. She gave Caspar a direct look, eye to eye. Ronnie and Caspar stood up, then embraced and shook hands. The chamber finally quieted down. Matters now rested in the hands of the gods.

The Chair worked through a speaker's list. Some were concerned about Philippa's end run around due process. Some supported keeping the programs, some taking up the Chancellor's line. After about an hour, the Chamber went quiet, unnervingly so. Ronnie and Caspar looked at one another. It was hard to judge the mood but it didn't feel good. The Chair asked whether there were any more speakers. None came forward. It was time for the vote. Simon was looking through his papers. At this point, Philippa unexpectedly got to her feet, and looked vaguely around saying nothing. Simon looked at her, a quizzical look on his face, but still she said nothing. "Dr. Lindstrom? " No response. "Philippa, you have the floor. Do you wish to speak?" Philippa looked up, coughed and started to say something too indistinct for the microphone. She stopped and gazed down at her colleague Dr. Sadra, who returned her gaze uncomprehending, and then across at Shirley who caught and held her eye for a few seconds. Then in a strong determined voice Philippa said, "Mr. Chairman, if I may, I would like to withdraw the motion on the floor for examination at a later date by the Faculty." The chamber suddenly erupted, people conferring, talking noisily, looking around. Caspar noticed Adsetts was motionless, staring straight ahead, as if not quite grasping what had just happened.

Ronnie and Caspar looked at each other. "Bloody hell," they exclaimed in unison.

Simon looked at Philippa and said, "Are you sure Dr. Lindstrom?"

The Dean of Humanities stood, rooted now and straight, head up, and said, "Absolutely."

"In that case I will ask if there are any objections, just raise your hands please." A scattering of hands went up. "Ok well, Philippa, accordingly, you will need to put the new question."

She thought for a moment then said, "I move the withdrawal of motion 2 concerning the deletion of the graduate programs in Ancient History and Aesthetics in the Faculty of Humanities from the Calendar."

Simon stood up, palms down on the desk, seemingly looking over his agenda papers, playing for time. Shirley in the front row was still staring across at the Dean. Then Simon straightened up and said quietly, "Any discussion?" Nobody spoke or moved, except for Adsetts, who had walked from his seat the few strides to the front of the presidential desk. He was saying something and gesticulating but could not be heard. Simon was looking at him, askance, hands on hips, and then slowly he shook his head and waved the Chancellor away. Adsetts stood for a moment, turned and sat down. Then Simon called, "The motion is on the floor, question, all in favour." Vicki counted the vote. "All against." Simon waited for Vicki who was adding up the numbers. After a few moments, she handed him a slip of paper. Looking around the Chamber, then over at the President and Dean, he declared, "The motion is carried." But not by many thought Caspar. "Thirty-seven in favour, thirty-four against." There was an upsurge of voices now as people were talking animatedly taking the measure of what had just happened. It was a minor uproar. Caspar wondered whether the Dean had sensed the energy in the room was weighted in favour of the primary motion and decided she couldn't go through with it. He mused that some senators would have voted for the motion in order to protect the programs named, at least temporarily, from being deleted. Others would have voted against the motion out of self-interest: better to scrap these programs than their own, or indeed out of a genuine belief that the programs were out of date. Some would simply have sided with the Chancellor who could not vote, and voted against. Some would have sided with the President and Dean who would vote in favour. This was all happening in the moment. Some would have seen the wisdom in Philippa's action. Live to fight another day or indeed a different battle, and voted in favour. Adsetts got up, gave the Chair a brief nod then strode out of the Chamber. Trouble would surely follow from this turn of events. Or, possibly not. Maybe the power had shifted sufficiently, things being put back in their place. The

University had stood fast, careers notwithstanding. A withdrawn motion, thought Caspar, might just disappear.

Caspar shook hands with Ronnie. "Rabbits out of hats Caspar," said Ronnie, not exactly smiling. "Rabbits out of hats." Now Caspar saw the wisdom of combining the motions. If kept separate the second motion to withdraw might have run into difficulties as opponents would then be alerted to the game plan and be able to rally support. Shirley was seen walking over to Philippa and saying something in her ear. They were both giving wry smiles. At that point, Shirley took back the Chair and called the meeting to order. Caspar and Ronnie left the chamber, meeting some of their students in the exit corridor. The students were enjoying the moment, knowing tectonic plates had shifted at least a little, patting Ronnie and Caspar on the back. Neha appeared suddenly and gave Ronnie and Caspar hugs. "I must say you guys, the women did rather well, don't you think," she said.

"I think a visit to the student pub is in order," said Caspar, to which there was no dissent.

The next day, Caspar sent bouquets of flowers to Shirley and Philippa. He felt much heartened. The University, thank god, had held its ground. But it had been a near thing. The President and Dean in their own regard, however, were not out of the woods. They both had to face the renewal process and be approved by the Board, chaired by Adsetts, and who knows what mischief might be wrought. But it's a funny thing. Facing down the use of power especially if it is being wrongly exercised is a way to get power back. But it does take courage and you can lose. But there was no doubt about it his female colleagues had stepped up. He was proud of them.

And so the semester went on for Caspar: teaching, working on his pictures, visits with Neha. He felt pretty good. Feeling himself beginning to pull away day-by-day, looking to the future. One thing he did not want was to pursue the academic life from the sidelines, living off past glories, the eminence grise. He wanted to create a new life for himself in the time he had left outside of the institution. Free, in other words. He wrote to Philippa, tending his resignation as of the end of June. He had an amicable meeting with her during which she said she was expecting it. She would keep his program going for the foreseeable future with three-year contracts. Caspar knew two very good candidates and said so. He would come back from Northumberland and teach his last semester in early summer.

# 39

Toward the end of November Caspar was looking for the thesis drafts. They came to him in hard copy as requested on the last day of the month. The work of both he found riveting. Beautifully written and well argued with supporting photographs, drawings, extracts from local historical sources and commentary from local people. Caspar noted on each various comments for improvement, but they were minor. This was among the best work he had received and in tune with the direction he had been pursuing himself, though not asked for or required of others. The award he had received gave him confidence in the philosophical respectability of his students' work. Neha's comments after looking through the theses had been right. There was something artistic in both works, voices creatively well expressed. He returned the studies with a note to make the edits. Then they could pass their work on to Jeff Matthews and Ruth Yeung by mid-December at the latest. Caspar emailed his colleagues and asked if they could kindly read the theses by the end of December and send him a brief email report on their view, concerns, anything that stood out as an issue conceptually, or as a central thesis argument.

Caspar had faith that Veronica and Cy would be ready to defend by the end of March. He would have to get the paperwork ready: approval to defend forms; names of external examiners; exam chairs, etc., in to the graduate program chair by the end of January, sooner if possible. The defence would be set for two months after that. Finding external examiners who would be at arm's length, meaning they had no personal or professional connection with the candidates and ideally, the supervisor, would give the candidates a good critical run for their money, being prepared for the hard decision if necessary, and not having some ideological axe to grind, could be tricky. The arm's length thing could be difficult in a small field. People did tend to know one another from long association. But even so, you had to do your best as supervisor to find examiners who could handle the thesis topic, understand standards were to be high, but able to be fair-minded.

# 40

Caspar's Rivers and Streams exhibition opened in the University Library Gallery in mid-December. The curators had produced a great poster from his toad photograph framed in landscape mode, and laid on wine and cheese. There was a good turn out from across the university, including Neha, Ronnie, Shirley, Philippa and the grad students. It wasn't long before pictures were being red dotted. The gallery kept a percentage to cover costs and required a donation of one picture, not leaving very much for the artist. He had already shown the works to Neha and let her choose one. The photographs were warmly received. Somehow Caspar had caught the wild loveliness of the Okanagan valley existing in water flow, lake depths, and mountains. His picture of the cougar by the lake in moonlight, the tree, and toad, among others were much admired.

Caspar invited Neha for Christmas lunch at his place and she volunteered to help him cook. It went nicely for them. Hard to believe a year had passed since they had become involved. Caspar gave her a necklace of polished local green jade stones. She bought him a book on trees based on the work of 17th Century writer John Evelyn.

The thesis reports back from Jeff and Ruth were as expected. Ruth asked for a stronger more critical explication from Veronica of the ways in which aesthetics could reveal the measure of destruction of ancient buildings. What was the aesthetic loss and why did it matter? And what was the effect on local people?

Caspar wondered about the degree to which Mao had succeeded through his so-called cultural revolution in cauterizing feeling for traditional norms of beauty in the masses. Imagine as a scholar or classical artist being sent to the countryside to work and be "educated" by the peasants. More was known now about what such people, including many Red Guards, went through. It was horrific. And, were the developers just too powerful to be stopped? How could the appreciative sensibilities be re-awakened and defended, asked Ruth, especially now that the lid had been taken off material wants and desires?

Jeff advised a strengthening of the arguments on the effects of ranching on First Nations land in the Nicola valley and provided a useful list of references for Cy. As they had to put their names to the 'Ready to Defend' form they had to be convinced by the work. Caspar thanked them both and said that their advice would be heeded and the work re-circulated.

In his younger days Caspar had believed that each academic discipline was unique in its subject matter and methods. Now he saw that all disciplines required form, creativity, and interpretation, plus a measure of artistry. Ideas were promiscuous. New subjects appeared through fresh allegiances. Disciplines mutate. Methods such as narrative become more widespread. As a supervisor you could no longer be an expert in everything, nor could committee members and examiners. But through judicious selection it was possible to put people together with enough shared knowledge to be a credible exam committee.

Caspar floated the names and cvs of Dr. Derek Nylands, professor of philosophy at the University of Toronto, with interests in the history and culture of the Canadian west for Cy, and Dr. Eugenie Cheung, professor of philosophy and Asian culture at the University of Saskatchewan for Jeff and Ruth to consider as externals. Caspar had had dealings with both over the years without ever working with them, and found them to be knowledgeable and decent. Once he got back the revised versions of the theses and all was fine with everybody he would invite the prospective examiners and if lucky, try to arrange the dates of the defences. The external examiners would travel to Vancouver and each would give a seminar in their areas of interest.

Neha was working hard on another book and would be teaching in the spring semester. She and Caspar continued with their weekends sharing much in their lives. Caspar was getting excited about his return to Jupiter. He reminded himself to take photographs of the farm to show Neha.

Cy and Veronica made the changes and they were approved whereupon Caspar, Jeff, and Ruth signed the forms and Caspar got in touch with the two likely externals. Eugenie Cheung was available for Veronica, but Derek Nylands was not. So then Caspar contacted a young First Nations academic at the University of the Okanagan, Dr. Melissa Walker, recommended by Jeff for Cy. She was a poet and philosopher and had grown up in southern Alberta. She was knowledgeable about the western heritage and native history, and had written prize-winning essays and poems about the rural life. She was delighted to be asked. The graduate chair in philosophy agreed to both externals and to chair the defences himself. Caspar had used him before. He was experienced and level headed. The defences were set for March 22nd in the morning for Veronica and March 29th afternoon for Cy. They would be advertised and open to the public. Copies of theses would be sent to the externals, chair and committee. A week before the exams the externals would send in their reports to be given to Caspar, the seconds, and chair. These were not to be shared with the candidates. The reports would highlight the qualities and weaknesses of the theses. The key sentence was always, "The thesis is ready to defend." That meant the work was found to be in good enough shape but there were questions to be answered. The defence could go ahead.

# 41

At that point, being the beginning of January, Caspar booked his flights to Newcastle. He phoned Cynthia to let her know he was coming. Arriving a week later on a cold and snowy day he took a taxi out to the farm. He gazed at the snow-covered hills, not by any means as steep and rugged as those of British Columbia but still bleak and daunting in the cold. At last he saw the little sign for the farm. They went through the gate, over the bridge across the Burn, and soon arrived at Ravensburn. The taxi pulled in to much barking from the dogs. Cynthia emerged in a sheepskin coat and headscarf and waved. She strode over and gave him a kiss on the cheek and a hug, leaning back looking at him, a decided glint in her eye said, "Caspar, good to see you. How are you? "

"Good Cynthia, thanks, lovely to see you. How are you?"

"I'm fine thank you. You'll be wanting to get in after your journey. I went over yesterday and got the heat and hot water going," she said, handing him the keys.

"Thanks that's very good. God it's cold."

"Well Cas, it's a Northumberland winter. We get them too you know not just Canada. Let me know if you need anything. I've put a few bits and pieces in the fridge."

"Thanks that's kind of you. Well, look I suppose I'd better get going. See you soon." With that he got back in the taxi. Driving on for a while he could see the slate rooftops and chimneys of the old farmhouse. He got out at the gate and swung it open. Soon he got the back door open and put the cases inside. The taxi left and he closed the gate moving quickly to get back indoors but pausing on the doorstep to look across at the little wood and farmyard. Then he was inside, grateful for the warmth.

Caspar could see snow covered sheep from an adjoining farm out of the window in the nearby field, many of which would be pregnant with spring lambs. First thing was to get the fire going. He had left logs piled up from his previous visit. Two of the out buildings were stacked to the rafters. Soon the wood was blazing and crackling. He put on some lights and looked for the scotch on the window ledge throwing care to the wind. He packed and lit Robert's pipe, dropping back into the old sofa. If only Marjorie could see this he thought. He felt the warmth and atmosphere of the farmhouse welcoming him home. There was some kind of psychologically comfortable fit for him here. The shape and touch of everything seemed so right.

The bed took a while to warm up. He was grateful for his flannel pyjamas. Soon though, he was asleep dreaming of Neha and the Senate meeting. Marjorie was there. He was trying without success to attract her attention. Next morning waking up early, thinking thank god for the heating. He could only imagine the frigidity of the bedroom pre-central heating. Windows frozen over. He was wearing one of Robert's green tartan wool dressing gowns with piping around the collar and sleeves and some sheepskin slippers, much needed downstairs on the stone floors. The Raeburn was blasting out, filling the kitchen with a soothing warmth. He opened the back door and looked out at the golden dawn light on the freshly snow-blanketed yard and woods and further east at the blue Cheviots. Tea was in order. He found the caddy and got the kettle going. Cynthia, bless her, had got him some bacon, eggs, and sausage plus a length of black pudding. He fried it all up with some tomatoes, made thick slices of toast smothered in butter and orange marmalade. So damned good. He drank his tea with milk and sugar as he ate his breakfast. He didn't want to move. More tea, then into the living room. Getting the fire going. He found the radio and put it on. They were reading the news on the BBC. Strange hearing the different accent and pronunciations. It really was another world.

Cynthia helped him with the papers for the car and by the end of the week he was all set. On his way back from a long walk across the land, passing Cynthia's, the dogs got going. He called them over, "Mollie, Rede, come," patting his knee. They did, slowly at first, then with recognition fussed around him tongues out and tails wagging, as Cynthia called them back. "Morning Caspar. Would you like some tea?" God he would.

Sitting in her kitchen, warming up, sipping tea, he was getting his bearings. "So how are you Cynthia?"

# 42

Caspar had a good week sorting through the different rooms in the main house and cottage. In between he drove to destinations around the county including Alnmouth, an old village on the North Sea coast by the River Aln estuary, and Hexham, an ancient town on the River Tyne near the Roman wall that crosses England from east to west. He was getting used to the Land Rover, which was the ideal vehicle for the roads and weather, and driving on the left. Changing gears manually did require some practice but he was enjoying it. He covered much territory, getting down some very narrow, winding roads, having to back up, learning where the passing places were, little indents to pull into for a tight squeeze, unheard of in Canada.

He particularly liked the road from Elsdon, an ancient village of stone with a castle-keep, or bastle as it was locally known, a wide grassy green and flowing burn, to Rothbury, a lovely old stone built town by the Coquet River. Most buildings in the National Park were of stone. The road was narrow, literally up hill and down dale, the countryside green and brown and beautiful, with sheep, dry stonewalls, hedgerows, ancient trees, and desolate high moorland in many places.

The A68 south he found was a wild roller coaster of a two-lane road passing through some incredible landscape. There were many long stretches of straight road he encountered, an inheritance from the Romans. Once, nearly out of gas, he'd had to search for a station, which were quite rare, or closed, or broken, or being filled. It could get desperate. He finally found one in a small village, using an old mechanical pump. On going into the garage office to pay, the man asked him how much had registered. Caspar didn't know so the fellow took his binoculars, and read the pump from the office — blithely non-tech.

Northumberland also was lightly populated so he often had the roads to himself.

In the second week of his stay Caspar received a buff-coloured envelope from the solicitors. He opened it and found a note from Patrick Willoughby informing him that Robert had asked him to forward a letter preferably some time after Caspar had had a chance to get the feel of the property and surrounding country. At that, Patrick wished him well. Caspar looked at the enclosed white envelope with his name written across the front by hand in blue ink. Curious, he thought. He tore open the envelope and pulled out a folded white sheet. Then he sat down and read the handwritten contents, soon sitting back in the chair not moving, just holding the letter.

Robert was telling him that they were half brothers. Robert's father, Caspar's Uncle Bill, was his father and had told Robert so as he lay dying many years ago. Robert said, since everyone concerned had passed on, he felt Caspar should know, though he had only come to this conclusion after much soul searching. Anyway here it was. At that he said he hoped Caspar was finding everything to his liking. He had always loved the place and believed Caspar would too. "I know," he said, "we've lived distant lives, but I always felt we were really part of the same fabric." He was glad to know he had a brother. Robert had ended the letter with the single word "love" and his name.

Caspar dropped the letter on his lap. He was having trouble taking it in. His mind was reeling, tears were forming in the corners of his eyes. He was in shock. His mom, Eileen, whom he had always adored, and Uncle Bill! This profoundly changed in an instant, of course, his own sense of who he was. He'd read about women absorbing into their own families children from outside relationships. In his case there was obviously enough of a family resemblance to Ted to allay any suspicions. Caspar breathed out, imagining his mother in a passionate relationship. He just didn't see his mother in that way. Did she give up her love to avoid family damage? Was it she, he wondered who had promoted the idea of emigration? This love thing, he thought, shaking his head. She'd had an extra-marital affair. Did she give it up not wanting to hurt Ted or the family? This was his reason speaking. Inside he was in turmoil. Did his dad, Ted, ever know?

Caspar decided to go for a walk. He was numb and burning inside at the same time. Did Robert know before his father's revelation? He decided to keep it private for now at least. No wonder he felt so comfortable at Jupiter. Could that be it? Were his presumed psychological similarities with Robert, with their shared love of art and nature, their habit of keeping notebooks, more closely genetic than he had realized? He had to give this revelation a chance to settle. Be absorbed by his feelings. It had left him feeling very shaken.

In the weeks that followed, Caspar, never forgetting the letter and its ramifications, came to the conclusion that regardless, Ted would always be his dad, the one who had brought him up and loved him. Given him confidence in himself. Watched his rugby games. Encouraged his academic ambitions. How he felt about Robert was too early to say. As time went by he got more into the groove of the farm, having high tea with Cynthia occasionally, and acquiring a growing knowledge of country lore, of being there, given its unique feel and experience. One great new thing for him was his trying out of the ancient public footpath system. The old signposted paths, going back to medieval times, that could be followed across country for miles, even through farmers' yards and fields. He could leave the paths and explore more widely on public or private land provided he closed farm gates and did no harm. It was great for the likes of him.

He walked miles along Hadrian's Wall. Followed the walks in the hiking book and learned to read the detailed Ordinance Survey maps. Now he was taking photographs. He discovered the many rivers and burns that flowed through the land to the North Sea. The experience ran deep in him and was curiously satisfying. Caspar found himself consulting Robert's natural history books and notebooks, which were a marvel in themselves. Illustrated journals of a life, a landscape, and a sensibility. There was so much for Caspar to discover and see including the many drawings he found in Robert's sketchbooks and his completed paintings, several of which he found stored in the attic.

At night he cooked on the big Raeburn, needing something substantial in the evenings after his daily treks. Sausages, beans, cabbage, and mashed potato with Dijon mustard became a staple. He invited Cynthia. They grew closer, more open and confiding with each other, there was more affectionate touching. He told her about his life in Canada with Marjorie and being a professor, books and his photography exhibition in the Library, which he showed her on the web, and now, his relationship with Neha and his decision to retire. She told him about life on the sheep farm, the winter hardships and mishaps, her married life, and bringing up her children, a girl and a boy, both now living in the south with children of their own, about her own interests in gardening and local history, and writing for a country journal.

One evening after tea over at her place, she had said to him, "You know Caspar, I can't get over how much you and Robert are alike. I know I've said it before. You have so many of his mannerisms and facial expressions. I feel at times as if he's with me. I hope you're not offended. I just seem to slip into it, without thinking. Yet I know you're not Robert. You are really quite different in your way, gentler somehow. You listen and I can feel you are with me when we are together. I've been so glad to get to know you and have you here, especially now." So saying she came up without hesitation and put her arms around him and pressed her cheek to his. Then looking up at him her head tilted Caspar caught a glimpse of the girl he had met all those years ago; he put his arms around her and pulled her to him, then they were kissing. She caressed his neck as he kissed her with more passion. They broke away looking at each other. He knew then he was going to betray Neha. There was an inevitability to it that

194

overcame his loyalty even though he loved her. This was not good, yet he found himself irresistibly in the flow of it.

They stayed together for the night. In some ways it soothed him, soothed them both, the human contact, the physicality, the intimacy. It was almost as if Cynthia was the only one who could help him given his surprising discovery and subsequent emotional bruising. Was it such a bad thing? Well, it was a betrayal and yet, the affection he received from Cynthia at that moment led back to a longing from nearly half a century ago and was indescribably fulfilling from somewhere deep inside. Cynthia was someone he had rarely thought about but now thrown together, they had needed each other.

# 43

Caspar reveled in exploring the land and woods around, taking photographs, making notes on the different trees and birds, getting down the banks of the Tarset Burn, eyes open for otters. He examined all the old farm buildings inside and out. In one building that opened out to the fields on the back he noticed a wooden box-like structure attached to a cross beam in the roof. How come he hadn't seen it before? As he walked around it he saw, sitting on a small platform, by what seemed to be an entrance opening, a large white owl. Magnificent. The bird, which he later discovered was a barn owl, just under a foot tall, looked down on him magisterially before launching itself silently into the air and swooping around, gliding almost, into the wood. Caspar was mesmerized. This was obviously a nesting box. He could see on the ground underneath and spattered on the stacked logs the dark lumpy regurgitations of inedible material, bones and such, from the staple food of mice and voles and possibly baby rabbits. He knew he would want to study the bird, and find out about its life history.

In the evenings he re-visited the rooms in the farmhouse, mainly just to be inhabiting them, feeling out the spaces, smelling the scents, looking through windows, lying on the beds, opening drawers, touching things, artifacts, and items worn by his relatives, including the farmer's attire of tweed cap and jacket, pullover and tie, braces and corduroy trousers. Interesting how all these items leftover from lives lived expressed a character, jackets that had taken on the shape of bodies.

Later he sat by the fire, smoked a pipe, had a scotch and read from the many books in the cottage. As he sat there on the old sagging sofa Caspar was thinking about taking on a nature project. He was eager to learn more about Northumberland, its geography, history and wild things. He could write and illustrate it as he wished, referencing his own and Robert's work and art. So different here and yet his impulses were the same: an appreciative loving gaze over the land and its ecologies, this, if anything, although he didn't yet know it, would be the cure for his blasted heart.

Time was passing. He had to be back in Vancouver for the two defences at the end of March. He felt confident for Cy and Veronica, but not overconfident. Defences could yield unwelcome surprises. At least Veronica would be able to stay in Canada following graduation, which would give her some security and a possible new life. They would both be able to apply for university level jobs. Then for him, a return to Northumberland for a few weeks before teaching his summer classes. This year he would be finished work by the end of June and retired. He would leave aside any decisions regarding property for now, even though he knew he would have to simplify things. Caspar wanted to spend at least six months at the farm starting in late summer. Experience the changing seasons. Fix things up a bit. Get to know more of the country in the Land Rover. Maybe Cynthia would lend him Rede. He would need to see how things stood with Neha, whether she would come out with him to Northumberland at some point. He felt sure she would love it and he missed her but now doubted she would come. She was he knew deep into her work and appreciated her freedom. And there was a lot to be said for it. Caspar had discovered he could also have a pretty decent life being single himself. But deep down, he missed the closeness of his married life. The daily sharing of small things as they cropped up, not just specific arranged engagements. He'd had a wonderful time with Neha and had felt things that he never would have imagined and his feelings for her were still strong, but now what they wanted from life seemed quite different. He doubted whether Neha would have the time for them to do much stuff together. Maybe he would have to get on with selling the farm so they could have whatever presence in each other's lives was possible given their situations. And yet the pull on him now to get deeper into this strange and beautiful landscape was also very strong. He was excited and beguiled by it and he could see plans and projects developing almost daily. Could he get a few sheep? And possibilities for writing and art seemed endless not to mention all the new hikes. He could grow vegetables. Look after the orchard and the wood. Get a few chickens. Appreciate the nature around and the quiet. He was sorry Marjorie was not here with him to enjoy it. Cynthia as his nearest neighbour, was becoming more of a presence in his life bringing over eggs, inviting him to tea, suggesting a hike and he found without trying they got on well in all kinds of ways. What a thing is the human heart.

## Author

Stuart Richmond was a professor of philosophy, art and education at Simon Fraser University, Burnaby, British Columbia. He lives with his wife in Vancouver. Photography, painting, and natural history are his main interests. *The Beauty Man* is his first novel.

# THE BEAUTY MAN

## Stuart Richmond

Caspar Ballantyne's unruffled life as an aesthetics professor in Vancouver is abruptly shattered by the tragic early loss of his wife. The book follows the repercussions of this event as he deals with grief and the surprising flowering of a new love. Caspar's professional life also undergoes upheaval as censorship from abroad threatens to stop his PhD student's thesis from proceeding. On the death of his cousin, Caspar inherits a sheep farm in Northumberland, and is faced with another dilemma: should he move to the farm where Cynthia awaits, or stay in Vancouver with the beautiful Neha? The reader is swept along as Caspar's drama unfolds, but is also charmed by sharp, precise, and often funny comments on nature, academic life, philosophy, and photography.

# Acknowledgements

I would like to thank Sharon Bailin, Robin Barrow, Peter Davidson, Rosena Davison, Diana Hodson, Margot McLaren, Jim Procter, Vicki Reid, Yaroslav Senyshyn, Christine Wallace, and Mandy Wallace for their helpful comments and criticisms on an earlier draft. I would like to express my gratitude to Rosena Davison who kindly wrote the novel synopsis. Thanks are due to Bruce Crowther for generously sharing his publishing expertise. Thanks also to the members of Vigilantes for their invaluable technical support and cover design. Over the years, my thinking has been much influenced by the philosophical works of Immanuel Kant and Ludwig Wittgenstein.

## Praise for The Beauty Man

Richmond has written a very highly readable and satisfying existential novel that travels to the aesthetic core of the human heart and the mind's propensity for philosophical capacities. In the protagonist's consciousness, we find ourselves immersed in a highly charged eroticism coupled with an intense understanding and nostalgia for the English countryside along with a synchronic polyphony set predominantly in British Columbian academic life.

—    Yaroslav Senyshyn

"The Beauty Man carries with it a timely air of ennui and irritation as its protagonist, Caspar Ballantyne, struggles through the decline of universities from being institutions dedicated to the pursuit and dissemination of truth and beauty to agents of social engineering. But, while Stuart Richmond neatly captures Caspar's frustration, a beautiful counterpoint is provided by the obviously heartfelt ruminations away from academia and, in particular, the evocation of the natural world of both British Columbia and Northumberland, UK. Those who still care for beauty and truth will love this book."

—    Robin Barrow

"This novel is a timely reminder that education is not simply about preparing students for work in their chosen professions but also about the wider and broader world of beauty beyond one's career. The author confronts comprehensively and with great skill the problems caused when funding for university courses comes from big business and certain offshore parties. He wisely sees the curtailment of an artistic and broad education as an assault on our humanity and our inner contentment. He does so through the beauty of dual loves, the one being the love of one human being for another and the second being love and care of our environment. In the former, the passion of lovers is sensitively tackled. In the latter, he does so through the natural beauties of the Canadian landscape and the wild, windy hill country in the farmland and moors of Northumberland in the North of England. This is a wonderful read. The nuances are not too subtle to lose the reader. The message of barbarian utilitarianism versus the gentle balms of art and nature is voiced with no punches pulled. The novel's message has never been more important and more current. I thoroughly recommend this book."

—   Peter Davidson


This book is a delight to read."

—   Rosena Davison

Manufactured by Amazon.ca
Bolton, ON

32680121R00122